Dear Reader,

If you ask any mother, she'll say unequivocally that she'd do anything for her child. So I gave my heroine a choice: she could muddle through on her own, pregnant and destitute, or she could agree to an outlandish proposal—marry a complete stranger with the goal of providing a secure life for her unborn child.

I've long held the belief that sometimes the greatest risks reap the greatest rewards. When Alexis agrees to marry Connor, in return helping him save his ranch, it's a risky proposition—and one they will both question from time to time. But in the end the reward will far outweigh the risk as they both discover what's really important.

The town of Sundre does exist. It's northwest of Calgary, Alberta, and I was taken with it the moment I drove down the main street. You could find a ranch like Windover anywhere in that vicinity. The area was settled by Norwegians in the late nineteenth century, and with that in mind I created Windover as a solid place that had decades of family history behind it.

I hope you enjoy reading Alex and Connor's story as much as I loved writing it.

Donna

Even knowing him a short few days, she sensed his integrity and strength. He would keep to any bargain they made.

He started to pull away. She stopped him with her fingers gripping into his arm.

"Wait."

He waited patiently, steadily.

"Trusting comes hard. Surely you can understand that? I can't afford to screw this up, Connor. I need to know what I'm doing is right for my child."

He put his hands on her shoulders, dipping his head to place a soft kiss on her forehead. "You wouldn't have told me that if you didn't already trust me," he whispered against her skin. "And you know it. It's okay to be frightened."

He was right, and it scared the daylights out of her.

"Marry me, Alex." The calm force of his voice almost made it a command.

She closed her eyes and jumped.

"All right. For better or worse, the trial period's over. I'll marry you, Connor Madsen."

DONNA ALWARD
Hired by the Cowboy

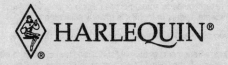

HARLEQUIN®

TORONTO • NEW YORK • LONDON
AMSTERDAM • PARIS • SYDNEY • HAMBURG
STOCKHOLM • ATHENS • TOKYO • MILAN • MADRID
PRAGUE • WARSAW • BUDAPEST • AUCKLAND

ISBN-13: 978-0-373-03954-8
ISBN-10:   0-373-03954-9

HIRED BY THE COWBOY

First North American Publication 2007.

Donna Alward can't remember a time when she didn't love books. When her mother would take her to town, her "treat" was not clothes or candy but a trip to the bookstore. This followed through university, where she studied English literature. She wrote short stories and poetry, but never attempted full-length fiction.

Her sister told her to just get out there and do it, and after completing her first manuscript she was hooked. She lives in Alberta, Canada, with her husband and children. When she's not writing, she's involved in music and volunteering at her children's school.

To find out more about Donna, visit her Web site at www.donnaalward.com.

**This is Donna's debut novel
for the Harlequin® Romance line!
Look out for Donna's next book,
which is also set at Windover Ranch,
and catch up with Alex and Connor in...**

Marriage at Circle M

**On sale in September—
only from Harlequin Romance®**

For Subcare—keep the faith. It does happen!

And with special thanks to Michelle Styles and
Trish Wylie for their unwavering support and guidance.

CHAPTER ONE

"Miss? Wake up. Can you hear me?"

The deep voice came first, then Alex's vision gradually started to clear.

"Oh, thank God. Are you all right?"

Alex's eyes followed the sound of the voice as she looked up, dazed. Trying hard to focus, she found herself staring into the most beautiful set of brown eyes she'd ever seen. They were stunning, dark brown with golden flecks throughout, large and thickly lashed.

Men shouldn't have eyes that pretty, she thought irrationally, realizing with a jolt that she was captured in the arms of the eyes' owner.

"Oh, goodness!"

The eyes crinkled at the corners at her exclamation, and she felt his hands on her arm and behind her back, helping her to rise.

"Slowly, now. You fainted."

Really? I hadn't noticed. I was too busy being unconscious. She bit back the sarcastic retort when she saw the genuine concern in his eyes. He even made sure she was standing firmly on her feet before releasing her—and then stayed close, as if he didn't quite trust her to remain steady.

He would have fainted too, in her condition and with this

heat…and the lack of air-conditioning in the convenience store hadn't helped much either.

"I'm so sorry," she blustered, brushing off her pants and avoiding his eyes. It had only taken a moment, but she could even now see him completely in her mind. Not just the eyes, but thick, luscious black hair, just long enough to sink your fingers into and slightly ragged at the edges. Crisply etched lips and a large frame in a grey suit.

Someone who looked like him was so far removed from her world it was laughable, and she avoided his eyes from simple embarrassment. She stared instead at his shoes… shiny, brown leather ones, without a smudge of dirt or a blemish. A businessman's shoes.

"No need to be sorry. Are you sure you're all right?"

She bent to retrieve her bag and purse. The first time she'd bent to pick up her dropped crackers everything had spun and then turned black. This time she gripped the bench for support, just in case. To her dismay she realized that she'd spilled her apple juice, and it was running down a crack in the sidewalk. She folded the top over on the paper bag, picked up the juice bottle and looked around for a recycling receptacle.

"I'm fine," she said, finally looking him in the face. Her heart skipped a beat at the worry she saw there. It had been a long time since anyone had been concerned over her. He was a complete stranger, yet his worry was clear in the wrinkle between his brows. Gratitude washed over her for his gallantry. "I haven't even thanked you for catching me."

"You turned white as a sheet."

She chanced a quick look around. Any passers-by who had seen her little episode were gone, and now people went about their business, not paying any attention to them whatsoever. Another face in the crowd. That was all she was. Yet this man…Mr. *GQ*…had seen her distress and come to her assistance.

"I'm fine. Thanks for your help. I'm just going to sit a moment." She coolly dismissed him; his duty was discharged.

Solicitously he stepped back to let her by, but once she'd sat, surprised her by seating himself as well. "Do you need a doctor?"

Alex laughed. Oh, she did. But a doctor couldn't cure what was wrong with her. "No."

The answer was definitive. By the way his shoulders straightened she knew he'd got the message loud and clear. Briefly she felt guilty for being blunt, so she offered a paltry, "But thanks again, Mr…?"

"Madsen. Connor Madsen." He held out his hand, unde-terred, inviting her to introduce herself.

She took his hand in hers. It was warm and solid and a little rough. Not a banker's hands, as she'd thought. Working hands. Solid hands.

"Alex."

"Just Alex?"

His eyes were boring into her, and she stared straight ahead at the office building across the street.

"Yes. Just Alex."

It wouldn't do to encourage him. In the early June heat her T-shirt clung to her, the hem on the sleeves heavy on her arms and the fabric pulling uncomfortably across her breasts. And what had possessed her to wear jeans today, of all things? Apparently such a heatwave this early in summer wasn't that uncommon, but for her the temperature only compounded the light-headedness and nausea.

Necessity had forced her wardrobe choice, plain and simple. Her shorts weren't comfortable any more, and at least in her jeans she could breathe. As silence fell, thick and awkward between them, the world threatened to tilt again. The feeling slowly passed as she took slow, deep breaths. "For the love of Mike…" she mumbled.

He laughed, a full-throated masculine sound that sent

strange waves through her stomach. "So, just Alex? Intriguing name. Your parents want a boy or something?"

"Probably." She couldn't believe he was still here. After all, beyond the first fuzzy moment that she'd succumbed to his arms, she hadn't encouraged him at all. His attempt at polite conversation had done nothing but awaken an all-too familiar sadness, the heavy weight of regret every time she thought of her parents. "My full name is Alexis MacKenzie Grayson."

"That's quite a name for a small thing like you." His eyes were warm on her and he twisted, angling himself toward her and bending a knee.

"Alex for Graham Bell and MacKenzie for the prime minister, you know? You planning on using it for the paramedics later? In case I faint again?"

He chuckled and shook his head. "You look much better, thank goodness. But you spilled your juice. Can I get you something else cool to drink?" His eyes wandered to the convenience store behind them.

Her stomach rolled at the thought of a sugary sweet, slushy drink. Every teenager in a ten-block radius had been buying them today. The very idea of them had Alex's tummy performing a slow, sickening lurch. She pressed her lips together.

"Or are you hungry? There's a hot dog cart down the street."

She stood, desperately trying to get some fresh air while exorcising the thought of greasy hot dogs from her mind. But she rose too quickly, her blood pressure dipped, and she saw grey and black shapes behind her eyes once again.

His arms were there to steady her, but she dropped her paper bag to the ground, the contents falling out as they hit the concrete.

His fingers were firm on her wrist as he helped her sit back down. "Put your head between your legs," he demanded quietly, and for some reason she obeyed.

Alex avoided his eyes as she sat up moments later. "Sorry about that," she mumbled, completely mortified at the awkward silence that fell between them like a ton weight. This had to be an all-time low. Blacking out not once, but twice, in front of her own personal Knight in Shining Armor. And wasn't he annoying, this Mr. Perfect Chivalry, sitting there calm as you please?

She expected him to mumble his apologies and hurry away. Instead he knelt and began picking up what she'd dumped on the ground in her haste.

Oh, God. Her humiliation was complete as he paused, his hand on the plastic bottle of pre-natal vitamins. His eyes darted up, caught hers. In them she saw sudden understanding. Now, of course, it all made sense. At least it made sense to *him.* She was still trying to assimilate everything.

"Congratulations."

Her smile was weak. He couldn't know. Couldn't know how her life had been turned completely upside down with a three-minute test only a few short weeks ago.

"Thank you."

He watched her carefully as he sat again on the bench. "You don't sound happy. Unplanned?"

She should end this conversation right here and now. He was, after all, a complete stranger.

"That's none of your business."

He had no cause to know her personal troubles. It was her problem. And she'd solve it. Somehow.

"I beg your pardon. I was only trying to help."

She grabbed the vitamins and shoved them into her purse. "I didn't ask for your help."

The pause was so long her scalp tingled under his scrutiny.

"No, you didn't. But I offer it anyway."

And who else was going to step up and give her a hand? She was alone, nearly destitute, and pregnant. She had no one waiting for her at home. *Home,* she thought sardonically. Now, there was an idea. She hadn't had a real home in a long time…too long. Five years, to be exact. Five years was a long time to be at loose ends.

At present she was sleeping on the floor of a friend of a friend. Her back protested every morning, but it was the best she could do for now. She'd find a way, though, she thought with a small smile. She always did, and had done since being left alone and without a penny to her name at eighteen.

Connor was a friendly face, and also the first person who actually seemed to care. Perhaps that was why she made the conscious choice to answer his question.

"Yes, this baby is unplanned. Very."

"And the father?"

She looked out over the bustling street. "Not in the picture."

He studied her for a few moments before replying, "So you're alone?"

"Utterly and completely." Despair trickled through in her voice and she shored herself up. No sense dwelling on what couldn't be changed. Her voice was again strong and sure as she continued, "But I'll manage. I always do."

Connor leaned forward, resting his elbows on his knees. "Surely your family will help you?"

"I have no family," she replied flatly, discouraging any further discussion of *that* topic. She had no one. Loneliness crept in, cold and heavy. Not one soul. Anyone she'd truly cared about in the world was gone. Sometimes she almost forgot, but now, faced with a pregnancy and no prospects, she'd never felt more isolated.

After a long silence, he spoke again. "Are you feeling better? Would you like some tea or something?" He smiled at her, friendly, and her heart gave a little foreign twist at this complete stranger's obvious caring and generosity.

"You needn't feel obligated. I'm fine now."

"Humor me. You're still a bit pale, and it would make *me* feel better."

It was a lifeline to hold on to. It wasn't like her life was a re-volving door of social invitations. "Tea might be nice, I guess."

She looped her purse over her shoulder. "So where are we off to, Connor Madsen?"

"There's a little place around the next corner."

She chuckled a little. "You use that line often?"

"I don't believe I've ever used it before, as a matter of fact." He adjusted his long stride to her much shorter one.

"I wouldn't recommend using it again," she remarked dryly.

"You're coming with me, aren't you?" Connor shrugged out of his suit coat and draped it over an arm. "To be truthful, I don't spend much time in the city, picking up women. Or for any other reason, for that matter."

He was wearing a white dress shirt that fit snugly over wide shoulders, then tapered, tucked into slim-waisted trousers. Alex hadn't believed men that good-looking actually existed, and here she was going for tea with one. One who had already seen her faint. She shook her head with amazement.

"So, if you're not from the city, where *are* you from?" Small talk. Small talk was safe and not too revealing. She could handle niceties.

"I run a ranch about two hours northwest of here."

"Ah." Well, she certainly wouldn't have to worry about seeing him again after today. She'd be able to look back on it as a bizarre, fantastical dream. A Knight in Shining Chaps, it would seem.

She giggled, then clamped her mouth shut at his raised eyebrow. "Is this the place?" she asked, changing the subject.

"It is." He held the door—more good manners, it seemed—seated her at a table and went to get drinks.

The coffee shop was trendy, and didn't seem to suit either of them. She pictured him more as a local diner type, drinking black coffee from a thick white mug while some middle-aged waitress named Sheila read the specials of the day. Despite his formal appearance today, she got the impression that he wasn't totally comfortable in a suit.

In moments he returned with two steaming mugs…one of peppermint tea and one with straight black coffee. The café didn't suit her much either. She usually bought coffee from a vending machine, or drank it thick and black from behind the bar—not that she'd been drinking much lately. Still, she was touched and surprised that he'd thought to get her something herbal in deference to her pregnancy.

"Thanks for the peppermint. It was thoughtful of you."

"I'll admit I asked the girl behind the counter for something uncaffeinated. And the peppermint might be, um, soothing."

He handed her something wrapped in waxed paper. "I got you a cookie, just in case your blood sugar was low."

Alex wondered how he knew so much about the biology of pregnancy as she unwrapped the long, dry *biscotti* and tried a nibble. It seemed safe. A sip of the peppermint tea confirmed it. "Thanks. I think we're good."

His shoulders relaxed. "I'm glad. I'd hate to have a repeat of earlier."

She laughed a bit. "You'll have to find another method for your next damsel in distress."

Connor sipped his coffee, sucking in his lips as the hot liquid burned. "You seemed to need it. Plus, my grandmother would flay me alive if I didn't help a lady in need."

"I thought chivalry was dead?"

"Not quite." His smile was thin. "And this way I can procrastinate."

"I beg your pardon?" She put down her mug and stared at him.

"I have a meeting this afternoon. I'd rather spend the afternoon shovelling— Well, you get the idea. I'm simply not looking forward to it."

"Why?"

He avoided her prying eyes and stared out the window. "It's

a long story." He turned back. "What about you? What are your plans for you and the baby?"

She took another long drink of tea to settle the anxiety brewing in her belly. "Our plans are pretty open. I'm working for now. Trying to figure out what to do next. It's temporary."

"You're not from here. I can tell by your accent."

"No. Ottawa."

He smiled. "I thought I sensed a little Ontario," he teased. "But there are so many easterners here now that for all I knew you could have lived here for years."

"Three weeks, two days and twenty-two hours," she replied. "I'm working at the Pig's Whistle pub for now." She needed to find something else, away from the second-hand smoke. But her tips were good, and she'd have a hard time finding a boss as accommodating as Pete had been.

He didn't have to answer for her to know what he was thinking. It was a dead-end job, and hardly one she could support herself *and* a baby on. She knew right away she'd said too much.

His brow furrowed a little, and she somehow felt she'd failed a test. Which was ridiculous. He didn't even know her, and they wouldn't meet again, so his opinion shouldn't matter at all. She was working on coming up with a solution. Just because she hadn't come up with one yet, it didn't mean she wouldn't. Heck, she'd been finding her way out of scrapes for years. This one was going to take a little more ingenuity, that was all.

It was time to end this whole meet-and-greet thing. She pushed away her tea. "Listen, thanks for helping this afternoon, and for the tea. But I should get going."

She stood to leave and he rose, reaching into his pocket.

"Here," he offered, holding out a card. "If you need anything, call me."

"Why would I do that?"

His face flattened and he stepped back at her sharp tone.

"I'd like to be of help if I can. I'm at Windover Ranch, just north of Sundre."

She had no idea where Sundre was, and had no plan to discover the wonders of Windover Ranch, so she figured there'd be no harm in responding to his solicitude by being polite. She tucked the small white card into her jeans pocket.

"Thanks for the offer. It was nice meeting you, Connor."

She held out her hand, and he took it firmly.

Her eyes darted up to his and locked.

Another time, another place. She lost herself momentarily in their chocolaty depths. Perhaps in different circumstances she might have wanted to get to know him better. It was just her luck that she'd fainted in front of the first hot guy she'd seen in a good long time.

And it was the height of irony to meet someone like him when she was obviously unavailable. She was pretty sure that being pregnant with another man's child was probably number one on a guy's "not in this lifetime" list.

"Goodbye," she whispered, pulling her hand away from his grasp.

Her steps were hurried as she exited the shop, but she couldn't escape the gentle and understanding look he'd given her as she'd said goodbye.

CHAPTER TWO

"Have you seen today's paper?" Connor stopped his agitated pacing and faced his grandmother.

Johanna Madsen looked coolly over the rims of her glasses, her shrewd eyes assessing. Not a single white hair was out of place, curled back from her temples stylishly and stopping at her collar.

"Yes, dear, of course I have."

Connor started pacing the elegant sitting room again, feeling fenced in among the classic furniture and expensive knickknacks. His head was ready to implode. How could she sit there so implacably, a study in calm? This was big. It was huge. It was probably the end of Windover.

"We almost lost the farm after the last scare. This'll put the final nail in the coffin, Grandmother."

"My, you are upset," Johanna replied with a tiny smile. "You never call me Grandmother unless you're piqued at me."

"Whatever." Connor stopped pacing and faced the elderly woman squarely. "I want to know what you're willing to do to help me save our heritage."

She laughed, a raspy, rusty sound that made Connor's lips twitch even as he waited for her answer.

"Our *heritage?* You've been thinking about this all day, I can tell."

On the contrary. For a few hours that afternoon he'd forgotten about his current troubles, focusing on another's issues. A slight girl with jet-black hair and astonishing blue eyes. With a baby on the way. Where was she now? He hoped she was still all right. When her face had paled and she'd wavered he'd simply acted, while no one around had batted an eyelash.

And even at her worst she'd still maintained a sense of humor. He admired that. It didn't take a genius to figure out she was in a bad way. For the father to simply disappear like that…Connor frowned. He had no compassion for cowards. A real man stood up and did what needed to be done.

And so, apparently, did Alex. Because the only sense he'd got from her today was that of strength and stubbornness, not hopelessness and self-pity.

And why, considering the current pickle he found himself in, was he thinking about her when he should be focusing on convincing Gram to release his trust fund?

"Connor?"

"Yes, Gram," he answered sharply, turning back to the woman who looked so much like his father. Right now her expressive eyes were troubled, and the mouth that always looked like it held a secret joke was a thin line.

"Look," he relented, "you know as well as I do why I'm here. There's already a ban imposed on beef exports. It's the same scenario as before, only this time it'll be harder to convince the world our beef is safe. Meanwhile I have a herd, a growing herd, that I can't slaughter but that still has to be fed and cared for."

"And you want the cash?"

"My birthday is less than a year away. Surely you can release it a little early?"

Her blue hawk-like eyes bored into his as she folded her hands in her lap. Hands that had once been rough and workworn but now held a small smattering of delightful rings. "No, my grandson, I can't do that. Your parents' will clearly states that those monies be held in trust for you until your thirtieth."

Connor cursed fluently; Johanna merely raised an elegant eyebrow. He glared at her, and she stared him down.

Damn it. She was strong—too strong. She'd lived her life, worked the ranch herself, knew what tough meant. She'd chosen comfort, a condo with a mountain view for her retirement. But she'd lost none of that prairie woman's steel.

"Gram. I can't do it. Not without the resources."

"You are your father's son. You can."

"He never had to deal with this." He said it and knew without a doubt he was right. The last scare had nearly bankrupted them, and they'd kept going by the skin of their teeth. But now…there was nothing in reserve. The only way to keep Windover running was with cold, hard cash. And it was clear now she wasn't going to give him any. His heart sank. He'd fail after all.

Like hell I will. His lips thinned with frustration and determination.

"Legally I can't release the money, Connor. You know I would if I could."

Her eyes softened just a little, and he saw the deepening wrinkles there.

"I don't want to see Windover go under either," she continued. "It means as much to me as it does to you. You know that."

He did know it. She'd spent all her married life there, had delivered his father, seen grandchildren grow and thrive.

"I'm just trying to find a way, and everywhere I turn there seems to be a roadblock." Exasperated, he ran his fingers through his hair.

"There is one other provision, remember?" she remarked blandly.

She couldn't be serious.

"The one other way for me to claim that trust fund is to get married. Gram, I'm not even seeing anyone! What do you want me to do? Post an ad at the general store? Perhaps I could find a mail order bride on the Internet!"

She shrugged, undaunted by his sarcasm. "Mail order brides have worked in the past, as you well know." She rose from her chair and stood, her five-foot-ten frame slim and imperious, but mischief sparkled in her eyes. "I suggest you get busy, my boy."

"Busy? Doing what?"

She laughed again, throwing him a flirtatious wink. "Why, courting, of course!"

Courting. *Hmmph.* Connor snorted as he accelerated through the exit ramp onto Highway Two. The idea was as preposterous as the old-fashioned word. Courting. As if he had time to romance a woman, entice her to marry him and have the ceremony before the banks called in their loans. Besides, who did he know that was single?

He came from a community where everyone had known each other from diapers. Most of the town women he knew were married, or on their way to the altar. There was no one he could think of that he would consider marrying. And if it got out that he was looking for a stand-in wife he'd be laughed out of town. And what woman would settle for that anyway? What woman should have to?

Nope. He'd simply have to come up with a different solution.

There would be government money—aid for farmers affected. At least he wouldn't have to cull—for now. But the aid cheque wouldn't be enough to cover the growing mountain of expenses while on-the-hoof prices cratered.

He could sell the southwest parcel.

Just the thought of parting with that spectacular piece of land caused physical pain to slice through his gut. His father would never have split up the farm, and Connor knew he couldn't either. Even in the lean years, during the Depression, when farmers had left their land behind to look for work, the Madsens had stayed and made it through. It was what they did.

He missed the sound of his dad's voice, and his strength. Oh, what he wouldn't give for that wisdom now, to sit at the kitchen table working through it. Together Connor, Jim, and Dad—they would have come up with a plan. Only now it was up to him.

He turned up the radio to drown out the thunder that was exploding around him. It had been stuffy, sweltering today. The rain would cool things down, and hopefully there wouldn't be any hail. He was going to need all the feed crops he could get. When you couldn't sell beef, you still had to feed it.

Connor sighed, wrestling with his tie with one hand while steering the truck with the other. He'd put on the suit to meet with the bankers—and, yes, he admitted it, to impress his grandmother. It hadn't worked, in either case.

Which brought him right back to courting.

Marriage was for a lifetime. Or at least he intended it to be. And as such it wasn't something he glibly approached. It would be a huge mistake to find someone suitable and marry her in haste. He wanted to be in love with his bride. He wanted it to be someone he cherished and honored and wanted to build a family with. And he didn't want to be pushed. He wanted it to be in his own good time, and when the time was right.

There had to be a way. A way he could bring the ranch back from the brink. His parents had been smart when they'd set up the trust the way they had. There was more than enough money in the trust account to keep things afloat while he restructured, figured out where to go next. If he were careful. But how to get his hands on it…?

"I suggest you get busy, my boy."

His grandmother's words rang in his ears as he headed north. What he needed was a practical solution. Something black and white and easy—something that made sense. What he needed to do was stop worrying and take action.

He envied the optimism that Alex had shown today… *"I'll manage. I always do."* Even in her dire straits she seemed capable, even though he knew she was pregnant and alone and without her own place to call home. She had an intrinsic faith that things would work out in the end.

The idea hit him fast and hard, and he almost steered the truck into the ditch as lightning forked in the sky ahead of him.

Alex. He needed a wife. She needed a place to call home for a while, and resources. They could help each other. He hadn't been mistaken in the connection they'd made today as she'd held out her hand and he'd taken her smaller one in his. They could become friends, he was sure. He could do her a favor and she could help him save the family spread.

He remembered how they'd parted. He'd given her a business card.

"Why would I do that?" she'd asked, and he'd known she was too independent to rely on a stranger for help.

But perhaps if she knew he needed her help as much as she needed his…

He changed lanes, steered the truck over the grass median, and gunned it out on the highway in the opposite direction, heading back to town. His heart pounded with anticipation and apprehension.

How did you propose marriage to someone you'd met only hours before?

The phone rang as Alex came out of the bathroom, clad in flannel pajama bottoms and a T-shirt. She answered it, expecting it to be someone for one of her temporary roommates. Instead it was the pub—asking her to cover a shift. Peggy had up and quit with no notice.

She looked out the window at the rain streaming down the

pane. The walk would be hell, even if it was only a few blocks. But it was extra money…and the tips were always better in the evenings.

With a sigh she agreed, and changed into a pair of jeans and her work T-shirt: snug white, with a picture of a whistling pig on the front. She gathered her hair into a careless ponytail, the black ends touching the top of her spine. For a moment she paused, watching as lightning forked across the sky. If she didn't need the money…

But she did. So she grabbed her umbrella from behind the door and made the trek to the pub in the downpour.

It was dim and smoky inside, and for a minute she contemplated the effects of second-hand smoke on herself and her baby. But this was the only job she had, and she couldn't afford to quit while she looked for something else. She had to eat. She had to think of how she was going to feed herself and care for an infant. Tying a black apron around her waist, she grabbed an empty tray and started cleaning up empties and taking orders.

It was only nine when he came in.

The door thumped open the same as it did a hundred times a night, but for some reason she turned towards it. When Connor stepped in, shaking the water from his coat and instantly scanning the room, her pulse jumped. It was too co-incidental. He had come looking for her.

When his eyes met hers across the hazy room she knew she was right. He smiled, a lazy, melting smile, and she braced herself. Men who smiled like that were deadly. And the last thing she needed was a distraction as lethal as Connor Madsen.

He made his way through the crush of people to her side. "Hi," he said loudly, over the pulse of country music and boisterous laughter. "Can we talk?"

"Hey, Alex! Table ten needs another round! We don't pay you to stand around all night!"

Alex nodded at Pete, the bartender and owner. Pete came across as all gruff, but she knew he had a heart of gold and a protective streak a mile long. It was one of the reasons she'd stayed as long as she had. As long as Pete was watching, she wouldn't have to worry.

Alex looked up at Connor with consternation twisting her face. "I can't talk right now, I'm working."

"It's important."

"So's my job." She turned away, heading to the bar to pick up the round of beers.

His hand was firm on her arm. "If you care about your baby's future, you'll listen."

That got her attention.

She stared up at him with eyes narrowed, curious despite herself. "Fine, then. But not now. Another time, when I'm not carting beers around."

"What time are you through?"

"One."

"In the morning?"

She laughed then, at his dismayed expression. "Yes, I have four more hours of being on my feet."

He followed her to the bar. Pete asked a question with his eyes, but she gave a slight shake of her head: *No, he wasn't bothering her.*

"I'll come back and walk you home. I really do need to talk to you."

She sighed. "Fine. But for now you're costing me my tips, in case you didn't notice. I need to get back to work. I won't make much money with you standing glowering over me."

She shouldered past him, pasting a smile on her face as she apologized to the patrons at table ten for the delay. When she turned back, he was gone.

At one a.m. they ushered out the last customer and Alex locked the door. Pete eyed her over the bar as he started counting out the float for morning. "Go home," he said, "and I'll finish this. That's the second double you've pulled this week. You look like hell."

"Gee, thanks, Pete." She didn't know whether to be relieved or nervous. If she left now, Connor might be outside waiting. If she didn't, he'd probably get tired of waiting around. On one hand she wanted to see him, see what was so important. On the other she knew it probably wasn't best. She didn't need any extra complications right now—her life was already full of too many.

She grabbed her umbrella from behind the bar and saluted him. "Tomorrow at four?"

"G'night, darlin'," he answered. "I'll lock up behind you."

When she stepped out into the darkness Connor was waiting, standing next to a bench beneath a streetlight. His tie from earlier was gone, and he looked sexily rumpled in the dim light. She swallowed, thankful that she'd spent enough time alone to have some street smarts. And to follow her instincts. Right now her instincts were telling her she wasn't in mortal danger. But the way her body was reacting to seeing him again told her loud and clear that she was in danger of another kind.

She should turn around and go back inside. She reached for the handle, only to hear the lock click into place.

She could handle this. She could.

"My mother used to warn me about strange men and dark streets late at night."

He turned, and in his arms was a bouquet of lemon-colored roses. "Then I guess it's a good thing we have a streetlight and we've already met. I can't do anything about the hour, though."

He held out the roses and she was too stupefied to do anything besides take them, the clear cellophane wrapping crackling in her hands. Where had he found roses after nine p.m.?

And, a better question, why? What was so important he needed to butter her up with flowers first?

Warning bells screamed through her head. Whatever he wanted was something big. She'd only received flowers once before in her life. It had been roses then, too, pink ones. And the gist of the card had been *Thanks for the memories.*

"Thank you," she said clearly. "But I don't quite understand what is so important you think you need to impress me with roses. Even if they are quite stunning," she admitted, sniffing the yellow blossoms.

She laughed a little to herself, remembered reading somewhere that yellow roses signified unrequited love. She needed *that* like she needed a hole in her head.

"You'd better get to the point," she suggested. "The novelty of these will probably wear off pretty fast."

"I have a proposition for you."

She began walking, and he fell into step beside her.

"What sort of proposition?"

"I want you to marry me."

Her feet simply stopped working, and she halted, frozen to the sidewalk. He *what?* What sort of cruel joke was this? Poor, pregnant Alex. Surely he didn't think she was that desperate! He could take his pity and—

Her head lifted until she looked down her nose at him. "I couldn't have just heard you correctly."

He grabbed her forearms, turning her to face him, his hand catching on the umbrella dangling from her wrist. "I want you to marry me." He huffed out a laugh of surprise. "That wasn't how I planned to say it, but there you go."

He wanted her to marry him. Her eyes narrowed suspiciously. What on earth? She realized he was completely in earnest. He was proposing to her in the middle of the street at one-twenty-two in the morning.

"I met you less than twelve hours ago. You're insane. Goodnight, Connor."

She turned to walk away, and made it a few steps.

"Wait."

The desperation in his voice caught at her and she stopped. "Wait for what? You can't be serious about this."

"I am. And I'll explain it if you'll only listen."

His suit was rather rumpled, and his hair looked as if he'd spent the better part of the evening running his hands through it. Against her better judgment she capitulated. He'd helped her this afternoon, and she felt obligated to him. "You have five minutes."

"Let's keep walking."

Shoulder to shoulder they headed down the street. It was considerably cool after the violence of the earlier shower, and Alex shivered in the damp air. Gallantly he removed his suit coat and draped it over her shoulders. If nothing else, all his actions said he was a gentleman.

"I went to see my grandmother today. I have a trust fund, but I can't access it until I'm thirty."

"So old? I thought most of those were age of consent, or twenty-one or whatever?"

"My parents set it up that way. Anyway, I'm twenty-nine. But I need the cash now."

"I don't see what that has to do with me." She kept walking, her eyes straight ahead. If she looked into his, all dark and earnest, she knew she'd be taken in. She'd been in danger of it earlier today.

She knew what it was to be fooled by a pair of beautiful peepers. And now she knew better than to do it again.

"This'll make sense, if you actually let me explain," he answered. "There is a provision. I can have the money if I'm married."

"I see." She didn't, really, but it was getting slightly less muddled.

"I think Mom and Dad set it up that way so I'd be old enough not to squander it, but that if I got married it would help me and my bride."

"Good logic."

"You're not going to make this easy, are you?"

She felt his eyes on her but refused to meet his gaze. "I don't know you, Connor. But I agreed to listen, so I will."

"Look," he said, with a hand on her arm, stopping her. "If I don't get some cash soon I'm going to lose our ranch. That ranch has been in our family for over a hundred years."

"Why are you in such trouble?" The last thing she needed was a man who didn't know how to manage his own affairs. Lord knew she'd screwed up enough on her own. But at least they'd been *her* mistakes to make and fix. What surprised her most was that she was already intrigued, instead of flatly telling him to take a hike. She couldn't escape the gentle way he'd helped her this afternoon. How he'd bought her peppermint tea and actually seemed to care about what happened to her.

"There's been an outbreak of cattle disease. It took everything I had to get us through the last crisis. But now...another case, up north. It's going to cripple the whole industry. Yet I've got a herd to sustain. A lot of farms will go under because of this. I refuse to let Windover be one of them."

She'd read the news, and knew the situation was as serious as he said. This wasn't mismanagement. This was a situation completely out of his control.

"You need some way to support yourself and the baby. What I'm talking about here is a mutually beneficial arrangement. You marry me, I get my trust fund, and Windover survives the crisis. After the baby is born, and you're back on your feet, you can do what you choose, and I'll make sure there's money in your bank account every month."

"A paper marriage, then?"

He sighed and looked down into her eyes. Yep, she'd been right. A woman could lose herself in those chocolate eyes and find herself agreeing to all kinds of madness.

"Yes. It won't be a traditional marriage. Look, it's not like this is what I wanted for myself. Believe me, I've exhausted every possible angle trying to find a way to keep things going. I'm looking at this practically. I get what I need and you get some help. We are both in predicaments here and are in the position of being able to help each other. Nothing more."

"Marriage isn't supposed to be a business arrangement."

That took him by surprise, she could tell. It probably did seem strange, coming from a woman who was practically homeless, single and pregnant. He might be shocked to discover how she truly felt about love and marriage. Not that she'd ever breathe a word of that to him. No way.

"I know. It's supposed to be love and commitment forever. And I do want that someday." His cheekbones softened as he looked away. "A wife who loves me as I love her, and children of our own. A partner to share the ups and downs with. Honor and strength, and knowing you're stronger together than apart."

A devastatingly sexy man with traditional values. Could he possibly know how rare that was?

"I'd be a means to an end," she confirmed, the words coming out strangled. She shook off his hand and started walking again.

"That sounds cold," he said gently. "We would be helping each other. I want that happy ending…and I'm assuming you do too. Someday in the future. We'd be doing what we need to do *now* to survive. I'm hoping we would become friends."

Friends. Now, that sounded dangerous. Her footsteps made squishing noises in the film of water on the concrete. What he was suggesting was outrageous. Preposterous. Humili-ating.

"I think you're crazy." She stopped outside a pale yellow house. "Thanks for the walk home."

"Alex, please. Don't say no yet, OK? Just think about it. I know it's not romantic. But leave all that behind and look at the facts, OK? You'd have some security for yourself and the baby, and a comfortable place to live for the rest of your pregnancy. Your needs will be looked after, I promise."

She shrugged out of his coat and handed it back.

"Don't you have a girlfriend you can propose to?"

"No." The answer was flat and final. "Take until Monday to consider it. I'll be back in town then. If you take the time to think about it, you'll see that you'd be helping me immensely. The least I can do is repay the favor."

It was too practical, too perfect, and too convenient. Perfect plans always ended up getting blown to smithereens and leaving her standing alone after the dust had settled. If her life had taught her anything, it had taught her that.

"Don't get your hopes up." Without looking back, she went inside and shut the door.

CHAPTER THREE

ALEX was zipping up her backpack when a car door slammed. She couldn't see the vehicle, but a quiver along her spine told her it was him before she even peered out through the peephole. Sure enough, he was skirting around the front of a huge pickup truck. She pressed a hand to her heart, trying to calm the thumping there. He was early. She had planned on him meeting up with her at the pub later. But it was barely ten, and he had obviously remembered where she was staying.

She opened the door before he had time to knock. Connor's boots halted abruptly, and they stared at each other. She didn't know what to say, and as the silence stretched out she grew more and more uncomfortable. She chewed on her bottom lip, while he stood so still she could barely make out the slight rise and fall of his chest as he breathed. It was like he was waiting to see what she'd say before he decided what to do. Offering her hand to him seemed silly, a kiss on the cheek presumptuous. She stuffed her hands into her pockets instead.

He was looking very different than he had on Friday. In a very good way. Long, muscled legs filled out faded jeans, and he wore a plain black T-shirt that accentuated the broadness of his torso. Her eyes darted upward; his hair, shaggy at the ends, was as tousled as ever. His forearms, brown from the sun, were lightly sprinkled with hair, tapering to strong wrists.

They disappeared into his jeans pockets when he caught her staring at him.

"Good morning." He smiled, but his eyes were focused on her lips, which she was still biting nervously.

"You're very prompt." The words came out more sharply than she'd intended, but the fact of the matter was she was more affected by his appearance than she cared to admit.

His jaw ticked ever so slightly in response to her tone. "I've got to be back by lunchtime."

Wow, wasn't this romantic? She rested her weight back on a hip. *Gee, honey, don't mean to rush you, but could you answer my proposal so I can get back to the cows?* He didn't say it, but that was how it made her feel. Suddenly she doubted her decision. Things were happening too fast. A week ago she'd just been trying to pay her share of the rent. Today she was actually contemplating moving out to a farm in the middle of nowhere in a bogus marriage to a man she didn't even know. This was so surreal.

"I don't mean to rush you." He tried an encouraging smile instead.

"You think by turning on the charm I'm going to follow along meekly?" Her eyes shot fire at him. "You need to do more than flash your pearly whites to convince me."

He stepped back, properly chastised. "I beg your pardon," he responded stiffly.

She couldn't help it. The whole situation was ludicrous. Her lips curved up slightly in response and she let her eyes twinkle at him. "I would think so."

She knew the moment he got that she was teasing. His eyes warmed, glowing back at her, and a reluctant smile tugged at his lips.

"It doesn't matter. I'm ready." She pulled the backpack out from behind the door and stepped out on to the porch.

"You mean you'll do it?" His jaw dropped.

She kept her smile in place. She was glad he hadn't been sure of her; that made what came next a little easier.

"Well, not exactly."

"I don't understand. Either you're coming or not." He leaned his right arm against the porch pillar, pulling the shirt taut against his ribs.

Alex licked her lips, unsure of how to begin. "I'm not sure marriage is such a good idea. We hardly know each other." She braved a look into his eyes. "For all I know you're some wacko, looking for an easy target."

His gaze was steady on hers. He didn't laugh, didn't smile, but took her comment seriously. "And do you really think that?"

"No," she admitted. "But this is pretty unorthodox, you have to admit."

"A business dealing, no more. I help you, you help me."

He made it seem easy, when it wasn't—not at all. This was her future and her baby's that she was tampering with. Alex, who hadn't relied on anyone in years, was suddenly considering becoming dependent on a relative stranger for her security and wellbeing. There was nothing simple about that. The one thing that kept her even considering it was the lack of choices she seemed to have lately.

She stepped back, putting a few extra inches of distance between them. "What I mean is, this is all happening so fast."

"I know that. Which is why I had an idea this weekend. How about a trial period first? You come up to Windover, stay a while, before you make your decision. If you decide it won't work, I'll bring you back here."

When the strain evaporated from her face like magic, he knew he'd done the right thing.

"I think that is a very sensible approach," she responded. Her eyes cleared of worry and she treated him to another one of her genuine smiles.

"I certainly don't want to chain you to the place if you're

going to be miserable for the next…how many months? I thought this might be a way to test the waters."

"Four months," she replied thinly. Chained to the place? The place wasn't worrying her half as much as being chained to *him*. And it would likely be more than four months. Once the baby came she'd need some time to recover; to figure out what to do next.

Suddenly her eyes narrowed. "How long a trial period?" She knew he was operating on a timeline, and a short one, and she didn't want to feel pressed to make this decision in the first forty-eight hours, or some silly thing.

"I don't know. No longer than a week."

Her breath came out in a rush, but her words came out cautiously. "OK. A week I can do."

"In that case, let's get going."

She lifted her backpack as he spoke, surprised when his hands took the weight from her. Her shoulder tingled where his fingers touched.

She'd forgotten his penchant for chivalry, which was surprising, since he was constantly polite. It was hard to get used to that in a man. Simply not what she'd been used to.

"Thank you."

"Where's the rest?"

She looked at her toes. "That *is* the rest."

"This is all you've got?" He halted by the door of the truck, his fingers on the handle. "No suitcase?"

"This is it," she said firmly. She would not, could not, get into a discussion of why her life was packed into a solitary bag. Someday she'd settle, find something permanent. Then she'd make the home for herself that she longed for.

Wordlessly he opened the door, helped her in, and put the pack behind her seat. Nerves bubbled up in her stomach. What on earth was she doing? This was crazy. Insane. She knew next to nothing about him.

He got up into the cab beside her and started the engine as she fastened her seatbelt. At least she'd had the foresight to do a bit of checking on him of her own. Saturday she'd hit the library and the computers there, looking up information on the man and his ranch.

Surprisingly, there'd been several hits to her query, and she had read with fascination articles regarding Connor and, more interestingly, his family. His father had been prominent in the beef industry, and under his hand the farm had flourished. The Madsen ranch had been around for over a hundred years. Now she understood why Connor was determined to make it through this crisis.

One hit had turned up a recent "spotlight" on Connor—he had done an interview on innovative breeding. His picture had come up beside the print, and she'd stared at it. He sure didn't look like some creep, despite the oddness of his proposal. He was twenty-nine, sexy as the day was long, and apparently smart and well respected. Her eyes darted to the imposing figure beside her, concentrating on the road.

She wished she'd found something more personal—a vital statistics sort of thing. Where was his family now? He'd only mentioned his grandmother. What were his interests, his quirks?

The only way she could find out that information was to talk to the man himself. She wasn't at all sure she could marry him, even if it were only a legality. She'd be stuck with him for the next several months. There was her baby to consider. She had to do what was right by her child.

Her hand drifted to her tummy as a current country hit came on the radio and Connor exited on to the highway. It was too early for her to feel the baby's movement, but already her shape was changing and her waist was thickening. It was her child in there. She hadn't planned on having children for years yet, and certainly not alone. But she was attached to this life growing inside her, knew that no matter what she wanted to be a good mother. How could she do that if she couldn't even afford a place for them to live?

Alex stared out the window at the city passing by in a blur. A trial run was her best option right now. At least it left her a way to get out.

The lane was long and straight, unpaved, leading to an ordinary two-story house in white siding with blue shutters.

Alex stared at it, not sure what to think. She looked out both windows…there weren't even any neighbors. No, wait. There. On that distant knoll to the southeast there was a speck that might have been a house. The land surrounding them was green and brown, spattered sparsely with trees. Basically empty. Isolated.

Beyond the house were outbuildings of various sizes. Alex, city girl, had no idea what they were used for beyond the basic "looking after cattle" umbrella. Another pickup sat in front of a white barn. To the side were tractors. Not the small, hayride sort of tractor she had been used to growing up in southern Ontario. But gargantuan monsters painted green and yellow. The kind she'd need a stepladder to get into.

Connor pulled up in front of the house and shut off the engine. "Here we are," he said into the breach of silence.

"It's huge," she answered, opening the door and hopping down. "The sky…it seems endless."

"Until you look over there." He grinned at her, came to stand beside her and pointed west. Her eyes followed his finger and she gasped.

She had focused so hard on the house that she'd completely missed the view. It spread before her now, long and gray, a jagged expanse of Rocky Mountains that took her breath away. They were a long way away, yet close enough that she saw the varied shades, dark in the dips and bowls, lighter at the peaks, tipped with snow even in early June.

"That's stunning." Stunning didn't cover it. Something in the mountains simply called to her, touched her deeply. Made her feel alive and strong.

"They keep me from feeling lonely," Connor murmured, and she realized how close he was to her ear. There was something in his tone that touched her. All this space…and he lived here alone. Something about him in that moment made her realize that he had a gap in his life, an emptiness he wanted to fill.

She wondered what had put it there, but was in no position to ask. And she wasn't entirely sure she wanted to know the answer either. She sure didn't want him to delve into *her* past, so she said nothing.

"Why don't you show me the inside?" She changed the subject, pulling her eyes from the scenery and adopting a more practical air.

He grabbed her bag from the truck and led the way inside. She took off her sneakers, placing them beside his boots on the mat in the entry, and followed him past a living room and a stairway to a large, homey kitchen.

"You hungry? We should have some lunch." He put her bag on an old wooden rocker and turned to face her. His jaw seemed taut with tension, and she realized that he was finding this as odd and uncomfortable as she was. Now, here, in his house, it became ever more clear that they were practically strangers.

"I could use a sandwich or something."

He took meat and cheese out of the fridge, condiments, and grabbed a loaf of bread from a wooden breadbox on the countertop. "I don't know what you like," he offered apologetically. "So we can fix our own, I guess." Silence fell, and to break it Connor began stacking meat and slices of cheese on his bread. He reached for a bottle of mustard, looked up, and saw an odd expression on Alex's face.

"Are you OK?" His hand halted, poised above his sandwich.

"It's the mustard. I'll be fine." She swallowed visibly.

He stared at her, his mouth gaping open with some sort of fresh horror, and a drop of bright yellow landed on his corned beef. He looked down, his expression horrified at the offending blot, wondering if it was enough to make her ill. God, he hoped not!

Connor heard her snort and looked up, confused. Her hand was over her mouth and she was trying futilely not to laugh. Before he knew it, he was laughing too.

"Oh, the look on your face," she gasped. "Pregnancy does make cowards out of men!"

Putting the mustard bottle down on the cupboard, he chuckled while she caught her breath. "Do you feel as awkward as I do?" he asked.

"Incredibly."

The laugh had done much to dissolve the polite tension that had risen between them. "I don't want you to feel out of place here. I want you to feel at home."

"I want that too."

"You'll find I'm easy to please, Alex." He smiled easily as he said it, but her cheeks colored. When he realized she'd taken what he'd said a little too literally, his smile faltered as they stared into each other's eyes. He became aware of the way her breasts rose and fell beneath her T-shirt. She was still breathless from laughing.

"I don't need much," she murmured. "A place to sleep and some good food. I want to try to help out in any way I can. I'm not used to being idle."

"Farm work isn't for you."

Her mouth thinned. "I'm not going to break, Connor. Women have been having babies for thousands of years."

"I realize that." His eyes didn't relent. "But you're not doing heavy farm work. There's a garden behind the house if you like the outdoors. I don't want you to be bored, Alex, but

I don't expect you to be some indentured servant either. Honestly, if I didn't have to cook at the end of the day it would be a gift from heaven."

Choices. Time that was her own, to do as she wished—making dinner or tending the tiny plants of the garden in the fresh air and sunshine. The freedom to clean, do laundry, on her own time.

Perhaps that sounded mundane and tedious, but to Alex it seemed wonderful. Growing up, she'd always envied her school chums whose moms had baked cookies for class parties, or who had invited her over for home-cooked meals. Not to be unfair, her parents had been great, but their lifestyle hadn't exactly been traditional. It would be almost perfect. If only...

If only it weren't such a sham.

Still, if he were willing to go through with it, the least she could do was carry her own weight.

"I'll be honest, I haven't had much experience in the whole domestic arena..." she waved a hand "...but I'm a fast learner." She went to the counter and began making her own sandwich of turkey and cheese. She took one look at the tomatoes and passed on to the nice, friendly lettuce, eschewed mayo and went for the pepper.

"All right, then. I'm going to take this with me." He gestured with the thick sandwich in his hand. "I wish I could stay and help you get settled. But I've got a couple of calves that need tending, and if the hands didn't have any luck this morning I'm going to have to call the vet. Will you be OK?"

He looked so apologetic that she couldn't be mad. After all, the whole reason she was here was because this place meant everything to him. She couldn't expect him to forget that and play host for the afternoon.

"I'll be fine. I can explore on my own. Go." She smiled and shooed him with a hand. "If you stayed in you'd just worry about it, wouldn't you?"

He looked relieved that she'd let him off the hook. "Yes, I would. I'm glad you understand. I want you to know…" His feet shifted a little as he admitted, "I'm happy you decided to try this out. I'm going to make sure you don't regret it, Alex."

She got the sinking feeling that she *was* going to regret it, deeply. Because when he was kind, when he was considerate, she knew she couldn't stay immune.

She followed him back to the door, watched as he shoved his feet in his boots, pulling up the heel with one hand.

"Your room is at the top of the stairs. Turn right and it's the first door. There's a white spread on the bed."

"I'm a big girl. I'll manage."

"I'll be back in around six."

At this point she started to laugh. "Connor. Seriously. Go do what you have to do."

He offered her a grateful parting smile, but then he was gone and the house was empty and quiet without him.

Alex went back to the kitchen and finished her sandwich, washing it down with a glass of milk. The morning sickness was starting to pass now and, still hungry, she snooped through the pantry and found a bag of oatmeal cookies. She grabbed two, then put her backpack over her shoulder and went to explore.

At the top of the stairs she turned right, but she was immediately faced with two doors. Did he mean the first one at the end or the first one right in front of her? She chose the latter and, turning the knob, stepped into what had to be Connor's room.

The spread wasn't white, it was brown with geometric shapes dashed across it in tan and sienna. He'd made it that morning, but there was a spot on the edge, just about in the middle, that looked like perhaps he'd sat there while getting dressed. The air held a slight odor of leather and men's toiletries, mingled with the fresh scent of fabric softener. She put down her bag and went over to the chest of drawers. On the top was a bowl, containing some errant screws and pins and what looked like a screwdriver bit, probably removed from his pants before they went in the laundry. Beside the dish was a framed picture. In it she saw Connor, much younger, perhaps twenty or so, standing beside a boy with the same dark hair and mischievous eyes. They each had a hand on a shorter woman standing in front of them. The woman was slight, with black hair, and she was laughing. In her hands she held a gold trophy. Off to the right stood their father, tall and strong, his hand on the halter of a large black cow.

So he did have a family. A brother and two parents. And from the smiles they appeared happy. But where were they now?

She'd trespassed long enough. If Connor had wanted her to know about his family he would have told her. And he might tell her yet—once they knew each other better. But she wouldn't pry. It was his business, his secret to reveal or to keep. She respected that—after all she had skeletons of her own. She backed away from the dresser and picked up her bag on the way out the door.

The next room was undoubtedly the one he'd meant. It was large, with a double dresser and mirror and a sturdy pine bed. The coverlet was white and lacy, lady's bedding, and Alex wondered if it was a spare room or if it had belonged to his parents. She put her bag on a chair beside the nightstand. After the floors she'd slept on, the dingy rooms with nothing pretty to redeem them, this was too much. Too pretty, too feminine. Too perfect. She didn't want to mar that pristine white duvet with whatever might be on the bottom of her bag. She took her clothes out and put them in the dresser. All she had only filled two drawers. A plastic bag held toiletries— soap, shampoo, toothbrush, deodorant. Those she took to the bathroom at the end of the hall and placed them on a wire rack that had one empty shelf. Other than that her bag only contained a journal and a pen and a picture. The picture she left in the bag, stowing the pack in the otherwise empty closet. The journal she tucked into the nightstand drawer, out of sight.

Going back downstairs, she decided then and there that if she were going to pull her weight at all she'd better get cracking. After all, it wasn't fair if for the next six months her only contribution to this arrangement was signing on the dotted line and leaving Connor to do all the work. He was willing to support her, not only now but after the baby was born, if only she'd marry him first. It definitely made her feel guilty, knowing she got the easy part of the deal. The least she could do was make sure he had a good hot meal at the end of the day and a clean house to come home to. If he wouldn't let her do any of the manual labor, she could at least look after things in the house.

Except she'd never done anything like it in her life. And now the fate of herself and her baby depended on her success.

CHAPTER FOUR

THE top of the fridge held nothing but extra bread and some frozen vegetables. *He's got to have meat around here somewhere,* she thought, and searched high and low until she came across a huge Deepfreeze in the basement.

She took out a package that said *"cross rib steak"* and remembered going to her grandmother's house when she had been a small child. Her grandmother had made this dish… Swiss steak…and it had been fork-tender, surrounded by onions and gravy, all layered on mashed potatoes. Surely there was a recipe book somewhere that would tell her how to make it?

She searched the kitchen for such a book, and came up with a small binder. The cover had a crudely drawn picture of an apple on it and the words *Mom's Recipes* in black marker. Inside were pages of handwritten recipes, in no particular order. Maple Chicken was next to Dad's Chocolate Cake. Bread and Butter Pickles next to Come and Get 'Em Cookies. She sighed as the microwave dinged out a message that the meat was thawed. This was going to take forever.

She finally found a recipe that said "Smothered Meat" and thought it sounded about right. Retrieving a roasting pan from a low cupboard, she put in the meat and then added water, onions and bay leaves that she found above the stove in a motley assortment of spices. She turned on the oven and slid the roaster in…step one complete.

She could do this. She could. Just because she'd never learned to cook, it didn't mean she couldn't, she told herself. All you had to do was follow instructions. It couldn't be that hard.

Potatoes didn't take that long, so maybe she'd really live on the edge and attempt something for dessert. Jazzed up with motivation, she grabbed the red binder again and flipped through the pages, looking for one that sounded good. These were his mom's recipes, probably the ones she made most often. She stopped at a page that looked like it had been handled often. Caramel Pudding. She read the recipe. Easy enough. Flour, egg, butter, milk, leavening, salt…brown sugar, boiling water. How hard could it be?

An hour later she slid the pan into the oven beside the meat and sighed. The instructions had sounded deceptively simple. However, they didn't seem to translate into her hands. She looked at the countertops. They were strewn with flour and sticky batter and dirty dishes. The first order of business had to be cleaning up this disaster zone before she went any further.

She was halfway through the dishes when she remembered the meat needed tending, the sauce thickening.

The mess doubled. Again.

The next time she looked at the clock it said four-fifty-five. She was exhausted, and with a whole new appreciation of women who willingly did this every blessed day of their lives. She was certain now that she'd had the easy job—waitressing, instead of being in the kitchen!

It took her twenty minutes and two Bandaids to peel the potatoes, and she grumbled that she was really going to have to caution Connor on having his knives too sharp.

She found a glass casserole and emptied a bag of frozen corn into it, put it in the microwave and let her rip just as Connor was coming in the door.

"Hey," he called from the front door. "How was your afternoon?"

I'd rather have been chased by the hounds of hell, she thought grumpily, but pasted on a smile and said, "Fine."

He came into the kitchen and sniffed. "Do I smell caramcl pudding?"

She smiled for real, the curve of her lips fading as she saw how weary and defeated he looked. "I found your mom's old recipes."

He came over to the stove, lifted the lid on the potatoes bubbling away. "It's good to come in and not have to worry about supper. Thank you, Alex."

Don't thank me yet, she thought, none too sure of success. The pudding seemed oddly flat, and she hadn't checked the steak yet. At least the potatoes seemed to be holding their own.

"Your afternoon didn't go well?" she surmised quietly.

When he sank into a chair and ran his hand through his hair, she knew she'd guessed right.

"We lost one. The other's touch and go."

"I'm sorry," she offered, her stomach suddenly churning with nervousness. He was expecting a great home-cooked meal after a rotten afternoon. He couldn't know she'd never made anything that wasn't out of a can or ready with one touch of a microwave button. She took the roaster out of the oven, and as the corn finished she drained the potatoes.

"Don't be sorry. It happens. But you know, no matter how much you think you get used to it, you never do."

She filled his plate with potatoes and a generous scoop of corn, then a large slice of steak from the roaster. The gravy was thinner than she'd expected, and seemed suspiciously lumpy, but she hoped for the best and ladled it over the top of his potatoes.

She fixed her own plate and sat down across from him. "I hope the other one makes it," she offered as he picked up his fork. Only to pause with it still stuck between his lips.

"Is something wrong?"

Connor looked up at her hopeful eyes and made himself swallow. The corn was still cold in the middle. "No, no," he reassured her, cutting into the steak. She looked so vulnerable, so eager to please, that he didn't have the heart to tell her.

The meat was cooked and tender, but the gravy…something was off. It was too pale and runny. He bravely took a scoop of potatoes and gravy and found a ball of flour rolling on his tongue. He smiled up at her, but he could tell she knew by the crestfallen way her lips turned down and her cheeks fell.

"It's horrible. Disgusting. You can't eat this."

"Sure I can. It's definitely edible."

Alex tried a bite with the gravy and made a face. "*Eeeew. What did I do wrong?*" She took a mouthful of corn and hurriedly spit it into her napkin. "And the corn is still frozen! Oh, I can't do anything right!" she cried. "You put in a horrible afternoon and then come in to *this!*"

"You *can* do things right," Connor said gently. He got up from his chair and took her plate. He put it in the microwave and heated it up more. "It's not your fault that I had a tough day. And you worked hard to try to make me a nice dinner. That was a sweet thing to do, Alex."

"Don't patronize me. I don't want to be sweet. I want to be helpful!" she burst out in frustration. "I've been on my own for five years and I've been outdone by a bag of frozen vegetables!"

He gave her back her plate, then heated his own. "The corn just needed more time."

"But I followed the directions on the bag!" She stared morosely at the offending kernels, now piping hot. Cooking was the only thing he'd asked of her, and the meal was a disaster. It wasn't a good way to start a trial period for marriage.

Connor couldn't help but laugh. "It takes a bit longer when you cook a whole bag at a time." The casserole was filled with enough of the vegetable for at least three more meals.

"And the gravy is revolting. But I followed the directions to the letter!"

"Where's the gravy browning?"

"Browning?"

He had to turn his face away to hide a smile. That was why it was pale. She hadn't used any browning. If he knew Mom's recipe, it probably said to thicken the juices with flour and water. And the lumps... If she didn't know how to make gravy, she wouldn't know how to make it without clumps of flour in it either.

"Connor?"

"I'll show you how to make gravy. It takes practice."

Alex pushed her plate away. Other than the corn, the taste-less, flour-pitted gravy had ruined everything. How on earth could she carry her own weight when he had to teach her how to cook? Never had she felt so defeated.

She scooped the odd-looking pudding into two bowls. "Do you put ice cream on it?"

"I'm out, but milk's just as good. Sit down. I'll get it."

He poured a little milk on the pudding and served it. He took a bite, sucked in his cheeks, and pushed the bowl away.

"I'm sorry, Alex."

Tears sprang into her eyes. She had never felt such a complete failure. Well, if this wasn't a whole new discovery. Alex, who always seemed to manage, to find a way, was com-pletely hopeless in the kitchen. The one thing she could con-tribute in this whole arrangement and she was a culinary idiot.

"What did you use to make it rise?"

"Arsenic." At his horrified expression, she shook her head. "Baking powder, like the recipe said," she insisted.

He went to the cupboard and took out a small orange box. "You mean this?"

"Yes."

He started laughing. "This is baking soda, not powder."

"There's a difference?"

"Oh, yes. If you taste your dessert it'll be sharp, and a bit bitter."

She did, made a face, and struggled to swallow the solitary bite.

"I'm a complete failure. And of no use to you, obviously. I'm sorry, Connor, for wasting your time and mine." She pushed out her chair, haughty as a queen, and made for the stairs.

"Hey," he interrupted, lunging after her and grabbing her arm. "One disastrous meal does not a deal-breaker make."

"Why not? You sure can't eat my cooking for the next six months. You'll starve, if I don't kill you with food poisoning first."

"Have you ever cooked before?"

"No."

"Then why on earth did you think you'd suddenly be perfect at it?"

"I didn't think it would be so hard," she murmured, leaning against the banister of the stairs. Tears threatened again. "Oh, these stupid hormones!" she said, frustration finally bubbling over. "I hate crying! I *never* cry!"

Thankfully he ignored the tears and remained pragmatic about the whole issue. "I know how to cook because my mom taught both my brother and me. I'm no great chef by any means, but I can show you the basics."

Alex took several breaths in and out, calming herself. She was the only one throwing a fit here. Connor was being particularly good-humored about the whole thing. Because of it, she decided to give him a little insight into her past.

"My mom never cooked much. We were sort of the take-out and convenience food house on the block," Alex admitted, not sure why he was being nice about it. "But I can do stuff out of cans and frozen entrees really well."

Connor laughed, and Alex smiled up at him. His eyes were

warm, framed by those shaggy dark locks. He wasn't mad. Not even a little. Even though she'd wasted that food and made a horrible mess of everything. Connor Madsen had a generous spirit, she realized, despite the unorthodox relationship they seemed to have started. He was certainly nicer than she deserved.

"You need this money badly, don't you?" she asked him.

He nodded slowly, his eyes swallowing her up in their dark, honest depths. Their bodies stood close together, and for a moment she wondered how it would feel to put her arms around his waist and simply rest against his strength.

"Bad enough to put up with terrible cooking and hormonal mood swings?"

A ghost of a smile tipped the corners of his lips. "Yes."

She wondered how long he'd lived here alone, and why. Why hadn't he married yet? He certainly wasn't lacking in the looks department. In fact, she was constantly having to remind herself to be practical—which was hard, considering she was already fighting attraction. She mentally added things up: his stellar manners, his consideration, his understanding and lack of a quick temper. He was the kind of man she thought she could trust, and more than anything that counted for a lot. Even knowing him a short few days, she sensed his integrity and strength. He would keep to any bargain they made.

"I'll probably regret this."

His hand lifted to cup her chin gently. "I sincerely hope not." Her eyes strayed to his lips, serious now, but shaped so that she couldn't help but think of kissing him.

"It's not forever, Alex. But you need to decide if you can trust me. You need to take that leap of faith."

"After a few days? No one in their right mind would make such a decision," she breathed, feeling the tug between them again.

"My great-great-grandparents met on a Wednesday and got married the next day. But you need to decide for yourself."

He started to pull away. She stopped him with her fingers gripping into his arm. "Wait."

He waited patiently, steadily.

"Trusting comes hard. Surely you can understand that? I can't afford to screw this up, Connor. I need to know what I'm doing is right for my child."

He put his hands on her shoulders, dipping his head to place a soft kiss on her forehead. "You wouldn't have told me that if you didn't already trust me," he whispered against her skin. "And you know it. It's OK to be frightened."

He was right, and it scared the daylights out of her.

"Marry me, Alex." The calm force of his voice almost made it a command.

She closed her eyes and jumped.

"All right. For better or worse, the trial period's over. I'll marry you, Connor Madsen."

CHAPTER FIVE

THE radio was playing softly in the kitchen when he entered, and the table was set for two, but Alex was nowhere to be found. On the counter was a crockpot. He lifted the lid and the appetizing smell of chili wafted out. His stomach rumbled in appreciation. She had told the truth when she'd said she was a fast learner. It didn't look like they'd have a repeat of last night.

"Alex?"

"Out here."

He followed the voice to the deck that faced west. She was standing at the railing, facing the dim outline of the mountains, squinting against the sun.

He stared at Alex. The deepening sunlight framed her figure, outlining her curves, and he was shocked to feel desire streaking through him like a current. Where in the world had that come from? Of course she was attractive—he wasn't blind—but he hadn't factored that into the plan. He frowned slightly. It had been a long time since a woman had had that effect on him. He'd been focused on Windover, and working things out, and hadn't taken the time to pursue a relationship. And he honestly hadn't considered how much having an extra person around would change things. He'd looked forward to being alone with Alex all day, perhaps too much. He had thought of how her eyes snapped and flashed as she angered, how hard she was on herself for the smallest error. How independent she was. But they'd made a bargain. And he had to keep personal distance.

"Are you all right?" Her voice was sweet and a bit shaky.

"I'm fine." He shoved his hands in his pockets, keeping back. "Dinner smells great."

She turned back to the view. "I found the recipe on the kidney bean can. I told you I could make things out of a can."

He smiled. "Mmm, progress."

"You haven't tasted it yet," she remarked wryly, and he took a place beside her at the rail, making sure their elbows didn't touch. He could still smell her, though, light, citrusy, and his nerves clawed at his stomach.

"Can we eat later? Let's take a walk. You haven't even seen anything of the ranch yet, and you're going to be here for at least the next several months."

They hadn't really had a chance to talk much about themselves, only about the deal they were making. They could be friends, and maybe, just maybe, he'd forget about how pretty she was in the late-day sun.

"Is it OK to leave the chili on?" Her eyes looked up at him, worried.

"That's why it's called a slow cooker," he teased. "Your meal will still be here when we get back."

They walked out past the lane and to the edge of a field, side by side but careful not to touch. A grove of trees and a fence separated the field from another meadow. Cows bawled in the warm sun as they grazed, their jet-black hides shining in the early-evening light, and Connor took a deep, restorative breath.

"It's part of you." Her voice interrupted their silence.

He exhaled slowly, surprised she understood so intrinsically. "Yes. It always has been."

"I can tell. It's in the way you look at the land. I've never had anything like that. I envy you."

Connor recognized the low note of sadness in her words and responded. "What was your childhood like, Alex?"

She stared straight ahead while he gazed at her profile. She was beautiful in such a simple, natural way, and she tried to be strong. But there was something in the wistful turn of her lips that made him sense the pain beneath the surface, and he longed to make it better. It had always been his thing, trying to fix whatever went wrong. But he knew better than most that there were some things you just couldn't fix—and he'd thought he'd left that protective streak behind.

The smell of fresh-cut hay filled the air around them, familiar and comforting, as she began.

"My parents were historians. We had a house in Ottawa. But we were gone so much…it was more like a base of operations. We traveled a lot."

She glanced up at him, her smile contrite as magpies chattered in the poplars.

"You said you were alone. Where are they now?"

She stopped, bit down on her lip, and squared her shoulders. "Dead. When I was eighteen they were going on a work trip to Churchill. They were taking a bush plane in…it's so remote…but the plane never made it."

So she was utterly alone. Alone like him.

"I'm so sorry, Alex."

She started walking again. "My parents were smart people, but they thought they were indestructible. They had little insurance. By the time I was done paying estate taxes, my lawyer, and their outstanding bills, there was hardly anything left. The bank took the house and I got an apartment, worked as a waitress."

She let out a long breath; that was all she was comfortable revealing at this point. They really didn't know each other well enough for her to reveal the nitty-gritty details. The loneliness. The longing for a normal childhood.

"That's my life in a nutshell. What about you, Connor? Did you ever want to do anything besides farm?"

He had. As a teenager he'd wanted nothing more than to be a farm vet, and he'd planned out his future like a roadmap. He'd work from Windover, and he and Jim would run the ranch together after Dad retired. And his family had supported that dream. He had taken his science degree and been about to enter vet school when he'd given it up to take sole control of the ranch operations.

"I was going to be a vet."

Their feet made whispering sounds through the tall grass. "So what happened?"

"I was home from university that summer. Dad had a load of cattle headed for the States, and Mom and Jim decided to go along."

His voice flattened, sucking out the emotion, making it sound like a news report rather than a life-altering personal event.

"They were a little south of Lethbridge when the wind must have caught the trailer. Someone said it looked like a weird downdraft, but we never knew for sure. Anyway, they went off the road. All three of them were killed."

His throat bobbed, suddenly tight and painful, and he was unable to go on. But he remembered that day as vividly as if it were yesterday.

He'd driven down himself. Half the cattle were injured, two were dead, and three had to be put down. He still saw the stains of red on the highway, smelled the death there. The cattle could be replaced, but in a single, devastating moment he'd lost his whole family. By the time he'd arrived they'd already been taken to the morgue. In a split second he *was* Windover. Everything was suddenly empty, like a colorless void. It wasn't right, working without Jim's jokes by his side, or his dad's warm wisdom, or his mother's nurturing support. They were just…gone. He'd never understood why he'd been the one left behind. Always wondered if he could have somehow prevented it if only he'd gone along. Instead, he'd taken the day and had gone to Sylvan Lake with friends.

His feet had stopped moving, and he was ashamed to discover tears in his eyes. Alex said nothing, just twined her fingers with his and squeezed. He cleared the ball in his throat roughly.

She understood. Their upbringings were diametrically opposite, yet a single moment in each of their lives had devastated them completely. He sighed. She'd been hurt as badly as he had. And he wouldn't risk being the one to do it to her again. All he'd need would be more guilt.

They turned back, the house visible, rising alone against the sky in the distance.

"I didn't realize we'd come so far," Alex remarked, and for a few minutes they pondered the significance of that statement.

Connor changed the subject, away from them and to the much safer topic of the background of the ranch. "This place…I've never considered leaving. Even my great-great grandfather stuck it out through a horrible winter. That's how Windover got its name, you know."

She left her fingers within his, a link between them on the path. "How?"

"He put up a rough cabin that first year. There was just the two of them, and the story goes that they were almost ready to pack it in when a Chinook blew in, melted most of the snow, and brought instant spring in the middle of March. He called it the wind over the mountains, and when they bought their first livestock it became Windover Farm and later Windover Ranch."

He had roots that went so deep. How could he ever understand someone who'd been rootless most of her life? She was glad now she hadn't revealed more than she had. They'd led completely different lives.

"Do you think we can go through with this?" she asked, angling a sideways glance at his profile.

"The wedding, you mean?" Connor nodded. "I think we are both realists. Despite the obvious differences in our situations, our personalities seem to match. Considering the predicament we find ourselves in, it seems like a workable solution. Practical. I know you have your doubts—anyone would—but if you'll let me show you that you can trust me…"

"Show me?"

The air cooled around them as the sun dipped further behind the mountains. "If at any time in the next few weeks you want out, I'll take you back to Calgary myself. Take this time, Alex, to find out who I am. To be sure I'll keep my word."

"But what happens in the end?" She swallowed. After two days she was already envying him his home, the one she'd always longed for and he'd always had. On one hand she told herself not to get attached to the kind of life she could have here at Windover, because it wasn't permanent. The other part of her told her to enjoy it, absorb all that she could and save it as a beautiful memory.

"I don't have all the answers. But, knowing what we know, surely we can part as friends in the end?"

"Do you think it'll be that easy? Going back to being alone?"

"Do you?"

The house grew closer with each slow step.

The thought of living alone now seemed dull and pointless, even after such a short time. It was a joy to know that someone was coming home at the end of the day. It gave the time she spent a point, a meaning. She'd have her baby when it was over, but who would Connor have?

"Who knows? We've both been alone for a long time. Maybe we'll drive each other crazy and you'll be glad to be rid of me." She tried a cocky smile, but faltered at the look in his eyes as they stopped at the edge of the dirt road.

He turned to face her, his warm gaze delving into hers, drawing her in and making her thoughts drift away on the evening breeze. His hand lifted to her cheek. "I think there's a very good chance you're going to drive me crazy," he murmured, his thumb stroking her cheek tenderly.

She stepped back in alarm, her face burning from the intimate touch and the clear meaning of his words. She left his hand hanging in thin air. A truck approached and spun past them, stirring up loose gravel and clouds of dust.

When the air cleared they said nothing, but crossed the road and made their way up the lane.

She woke at dawn and checked her watch. It was barely five. Squinting, she glared at the window that was letting in all the lemony fresh sunshine. Last night she'd been so distracted she'd forgotten to pull the blinds. Her cheek still remembered the weight of his hand, caressing the soft skin there. Her drive him crazy? Not if he drove her nuts first. He was giving her the opportunity to back out. And she should. She was far too taken with him already. He was too strong, yet kind and understanding.

And he looked far too good in a pair of faded jeans. Add in that messy, slightly ragged hair, and any woman would be a goner. She should run, very quickly, in the opposite direction.

But the truth of the matter was this was by far the best way for her to provide for her child. She couldn't go back to where she'd been staying, as the tenant had decided to move in with her boyfriend when Alex left. She'd quit her job at a moment's notice. And now was no time to start from scratch.

She stared at the window. The flimsy white curtains didn't do much to keep out daylight, even when the sun was rising on the other side of the house. Tonight she'd make sure the blind was down. She sure didn't want to wake at five every day.

Footsteps passed outside her door, quiet, stocking-footed. A floorboard creaked beneath the weight. Connor was up already? She pushed the covers back and stepped out onto the hardwood floor. She'd missed his rising yesterday. She might as well get up now that she was awake, start learning what he liked for breakfast—and how he cooked it. If she weren't going to be allowed to help *outside,* she meant to do her best *inside.*

She went downstairs dressed still in her pajamas—cotton shorts and a tank top. When she reached the kitchen, Connor already had a skillet on the burner and was half buried in the refrigerator, pulling out ingredients. He was dressed in what she now realized must be his customary uniform—faded jeans and a plain T-shirt. Her mouth grew dry as he dug deeper, the seat of his jeans filling out. She was in serious trouble here.

The touch of his hand on her face last night had prompted strange dreams. In them he'd stroked her cheek and kissed her. And it hadn't been a brotherly kiss either. In her slumbers he'd taken her mouth wholly, completely. His lips had been soft, deliberate, and devastating. His hands had glided over her skin. Tender. Possessive.

He straightened, turned with eggs in his hands, and jumped.

She wanted to disappear through the floor. Belatedly she realized her fingers were touching her lips…and that her nipples were puckered up almost painfully. All from the sight of his bottom in some worn denim.

"I didn't expect you up for hours yet."

Blushing, she turned away, searching the cupboard for dishes. *Hormones,* she tried, quite unsuccessfully, to convince herself. It had to be the excess hormones in her system making her feel so…carnal.

"I forgot to pull the blind last night," she said to the plates. "You always up this early?"

He put a carton of eggs on the counter and nodded. "Ranching isn't exactly a nine-to-five business. You hungry?"

She was ravenous…and she couldn't blame *that* on her pregnancy. She'd found it incredibly difficult to eat after their walk, despite the fact that the chili had actually turned out fine.

"Normally I don't eat until later, but after last night…"

The words hung between them, not only a reminder of their walk but of the strange feeling of intimacy that had followed their personal revelations. She needed to keep things casual. She'd walked away from his touch last night; he had no idea she'd started fantasizing about him. She didn't want things to become more uncomfortable between them.

"What are you making?" She asked it quickly, to dispel the sudden feeling that he was remembering too.

"Scrambled eggs, sliced ham, and toast."

"Will you show me?" She stepped forward, feeling a little silly that at twenty-three she didn't even know how to scramble eggs. She wanted desperately to contribute, but having Connor have to show her everything…he could probably do it much faster himself than taking the time to instruct her. Setting her jaw, she vowed to pay close attention and learn—quickly.

"Sure." He cracked eggs into a bowl and handed her a whisk while he put butter in the pan. "Here. Beat the daylights out of those for a minute."

Her lips curved up without warning. She was really starting to like his sense of humor. He was relaxed and joking, which meant he wasn't letting what had happened affect their relationship. Perhaps being married, even for such a brief time, could be enjoyable. Their personalities meshed. And, yes, the ranch was isolated, but Alex was used to being alone and didn't find it too solitary. For the first time in a long time she felt a little hope that things would turn out all right after all. If only she could learn her share. If only they could maintain their boundaries.

As she was whisking he explained about adding salt and pepper and she paid close attention to quantities. He let the butter melt in the skillet, and then poured in the eggs.

"Once they start to set a little, then you keep pushing them around," he explained, and handed her the spatula.

She stuck it in the pan but splashed a little egg batter over the side. "Like this," he explained, and moved in behind her, covering her hand with his own on the spatula.

Alex's breath caught. Connor had showered last night and now, at the start of day, the scent of his soap was mingled with the smell of man in the morning. His body was warm and firm, close behind her, and the intimacy of the moment curled through her. OK, maybe this marriage wouldn't be as enjoyable as she thought. Not if she had to spend the next several months hiding the fact that he made her pulse race every time he was close. Last night's tender caress was only the tip of the iceberg.

His voice was oddly thick as he pulled away. "You're getting it now," he mumbled, and moved to put slices of bread in the toaster.

She pushed the eggs to one side and managed to fry the ham slices without incident. Silently they sat at the table to eat, while the light around them grew brighter.

"I called my grandmother last night."

She nearly choked on her toast. "You did?"

"I explained I was getting married." His smile was grim. "I think she'll probably come up here today to check you out."

She hadn't counted on grandmothers. And his had to know that this wasn't a regular marriage. This had been a real, functioning family, she was sure. And that meant that his grandmother would likely be outraged at the fact that he was marrying a relative stranger for money.

"Why did you do that? I didn't sign up for irate grandmothers!" Her voice rose in panic. Not only was she a stranger, but an inept one. She didn't know much about being domestic and less about farming. Surely his grandmother would find her completely unsuitable? Alex wasn't ready for that type of criticism to be heaped on her head. After the ridiculous sexual thoughts she'd had about him lately, she couldn't seem to keep up with all the emotions he inspired in her. Last night had been sympathy, tenderness. Then carnality, embarrassment. And right now she was seeing the red cape of anger. If this was going to be a rollercoaster, she wanted off.

Connor didn't see the huge problem in telling his grandmother anything at all. After all, Gram had told him to get courting. Perhaps she hadn't meant quite this quickly, but Johanna Madsen was a practical woman. She'd figure out the truth very quickly. She was the one who had put him in this position, so she could say nothing about how he handled it.

Thankfully, he knew that Gram wasn't too hung up on conventionalities. But, more than that, Gram was the only family he had left. His honor, his family loyalty, demanded he be honest and upfront about it.

"She's all I have, Alex." He studied the ornery set of Alex's chin and smiled at her stubbornness. In the light of early morning she was beautiful, without artifice. All that was amplified when her eyes snapped with anger and her cheeks flushed. Perhaps it was the pregnancy, but her skin had a luminescence— and he'd caught sight of lots of it when she'd arrived in her pjs.

Yet she wasn't soft. There was a strength, a resolution about her that he admired. Alex Grayson was no pushover…and Gram would respect that if nothing else.

"Gram's pretty gruff, but she loves me and understands what's going on. Not only that, but if we're going to move ahead with this then it only makes sense that you meet my family right away. The most important thing to remember is she hates deception. She's way too smart for that, and will see through you like anything."

Alex put down her fork, her lips contorted grimly. "So you automatically think I'll lie to her? Thanks a lot."

"Of course not. That's not what I meant!"

"It sounded pretty clear to me." She gave up all pretence of eating. "Do you want me to tell her exactly why I'm here?

Because I got knocked up by a low-life, have no prospects, and latched on to you for your money?"

"That's not exactly how I'd put it, no. Besides, I asked you."

"Like that'll matter. Does she even know I'm pregnant?"

"No." Surprising Gram with a fiancée last night had been enough, Connor thought. They'd get to the baby in time. After the wedding would be time enough to tell Gram that there would be a third Madsen in the household before long.

He swallowed roughly. Only the baby wouldn't be a Madsen. How could he have forgotten that?

"She's naturally going to think I'm a gold-digger. Thanks a lot, Connor."

She took her plate to the sink, nausea suddenly battling with her anger. At this rate she wouldn't have to worry about baby weight gain. She was always in such a tumult that she never seemed to finish a meal!

Bracing one hand on the counter, she closed her eyes, willing away the sickness. When she spoke, her words were soft and accusing.

"Isn't not telling her a form of deception?"

"I'm going to tell her, of course," he countered. "It's not exactly something we can keep hidden. I thought I'd give her a little time to get used to the marriage idea first."

"Coward," she mumbled.

"I beg your pardon?"

Alex scraped her plate into the garbage. "I can't believe you're afraid of your granny," she accused.

"I'm not a coward for not hitting her with all the details at once," he defended. "I did nothing wrong by letting my grandmother know we're getting married."

He frowned as he looked at her lips, thinned into a condemning line. Great. If she were this upset about meeting his grandmother, she was going to go ballistic when he told her the rest of the news.

"Unfortunately, I have an association meeting in Red Deer this morning. I'll be gone most of the day. Remember what I told you and you'll be fine. Just be yourself, Alex, and be honest, and I'm sure she'll love you." It was paltry pacification and it failed miserably.

"So you're lighting the fire and leaving me to put it out? Last night you said for me to trust you. Then you pull something like this. You didn't even *consult* me. Did you seriously think I'd be OK with this?"

"I honestly didn't think it'd be this big of a deal. I'm still not completely sure why it is."

"Oh, it's a big deal. *Huge.* Today I get to be judged. *Alone.*"

For a moment he considered skipping the meeting. He hadn't considered how upset she might be over it, and in hindsight he probably should have talked to her first before calling Gram. But he'd been disconcerted after their talk last night, and he hadn't considered all the ramifications. And he'd learned something new—something that surprised him. Going toe-to-toe with Alex was invigorating. When they argued they left all pretence and awkwardness behind. They were *honest.* It was liberating.

Alex sighed, a mixture of frustration and resignation. "I'd better get started tidying this place up, then."

He took his empty plate to the sink. She was furious. It was in the way her eyes refused to even glance in his direction, in the icy set of her cheek. It shouldn't matter, but it did. Despite how *alive* she looked when she was wound up, he didn't like being at outs with her.

"I'm sorry, Alex. I certainly didn't intend to upset you. With any luck I'll be back by lunch, and she won't be here yet. Or I can make a few phone calls. Maybe I can reschedule the meeting, and then we can face her together."

She turned, raised her chin defiantly.

"I can handle your grandmother," she retorted. "It's the fact that I have to that I don't like."

"Point taken."

"If you want me to stay, don't let it happen again."

He couldn't help but smile a bit at her steel. She might be down but she would never admit to being out. The more they talked, the more he realized how resilient she was. He wondered what she'd left out about her life last night during their walk. "Agreed."

He stepped closer to her and laid a hand on her cheek. A few tendrils curled around her face and whispered against the rough skin of his hand. Her hair... He'd resisted the temptation thus far to sink his hands into that rich carpet of darkness. But this morning it was out of her customary ponytail and rippled down her back. There wasn't a man in this hemisphere who could resist hair like that.

"I'm sorry I didn't think this through better." He made the apology clear. "But, Alex?" At the questioning look in her eyes he smiled. "You're amazing. I don't think I've ever seen a woman more determined than you. You'll be great."

He pressed a kiss of reassurance to her forehead as he left for his chores. He'd lied. He'd met one woman more determined...and Alex was going to meet her too, very soon.

CHAPTER SIX

THE eggs and ham, what she'd managed to eat of them, stayed down. Alex showered, dressed in clean jeans and T-shirt, and wished she had something nicer to wear. Grandmothers were not on her top ten list of things she wanted to do today. Alex knew that if she didn't pass muster, chances were the wedding would never take place.

She fussed with the hem of her shirt. Well, there was nothing she could do about her dearth of a wardrobe. Instead she went to work, tidying the house, dusting and vacuuming, and making sure the appliances gleamed. She took pleasure in looking in at the rooms, tidy and shining. It felt... already... like a home.

She frowned. Two days. Two days and she was thinking of this as home. She had to be careful and remember that this was temporary. If she got too invested, then she was only setting herself up for heartache when it became time to leave. And leave she must. They would go their separate ways, and she would find a new place for herself and the baby she'd be bringing up alone.

But first she had to deal with Connor's grandmother. The fact that she had to made her blood boil. Of all the nerve. Connor had sat there, calm as you please, and just *announced* that he'd told his grandmother about their plans. Now he was off "working", and she was left to deal with the fallout alone. How typically male!

She'd get lots of mileage out of this one. He owed her big time for dropping this on her and leaving.

She was heading upstairs when a horrible thought took hold. What if the revered lady arrived expecting to spend the night? Was Alex already in the room she would expect to occupy? Would his grandmother be expecting her to be sharing Connor's bed?

The thought of sleeping next to Connor all night made her stomach roll over. It was bad enough the tricks her mind was playing on her; she wasn't sure how she could handle lying close to his body through the night, listening to his steady breath, feeling his warmth. She had no business feeling this elemental attraction to him, not when their relationship was temporary and she was pregnant. And who knew what would happen while they were sleeping? She was apt to wake up draped over him, and how embarrassing would that be? As if Connor would be attracted to her—poor, plain Alex, pregnant with another man's child. Briefly she remembered how gently he'd touched her last night, and her stomach twisted again. Maybe it was possible that he was attracted, she supposed, but someone had to keep a clear head around here!

She could switch her things to the other spare room. It wouldn't take but a moment, and then Mrs. Madsen could have the white room. She was just taking the steps with fresh linens in her hands when the doorbell rang. Her heart sank. She'd run out of time.

She put the linens on a chair and opened the door with a heavy and panicked heart.

"You must be Alexis. I'm Johanna Madsen, Connor's grandmother."

Of course you are. Alex held the thought inside and tried to keep her mouth from dropping open. The woman was tall and imperious, dressed in a stylish black pantsuit with a real silk scarf twined about her neck.

But she was looking at Alex in a friendly, grandmotherly sort of way, not with the glare of suspicion and dislike that Alex had completely expected.

"Please, come in," Alex said automatically, then felt ridiculous. Johanna belonged here so much more than she did!

Alex stepped aside and Johanna came in, pulling a suitcase behind her. Alex's heart sank. Johanna *was* planning on staying.

"Connor's gone to a meeting," she said haltingly, hating the uncertainty in her voice.

Johanna's brow crinkled in the middle. "All this fuss—all these meetings he has to attend when there's hay to be cut. It looks like a good crop. He'll need it."

"He will?"

Johanna smiled at Alex indulgently, making Alex feel like a simple child. "When you can't sell beef, you've got to feed the ones you've got." She put a friendly hand on Alex's shoulder. "Let's have tea."

Alex was helpless to do anything but follow Johanna into the kitchen. The woman had been in the house less than five minutes and already she was in charge. Alex wasn't sure whether to be offended or strangely relieved as she paused in the doorway to the kitchen, unsure of what to do.

Johanna placed the kettle on the burner, and then knelt down with her head in the cupboard, searching for teabags. A rancher's wife, born and bred. It made Alex feel even more like an impostor.

"So, when are you due, Alexis?"

Alex's mouth *did* drop open then, and she stood paralyzed. Johanna took the kettle off the burner and poured, unhesitating in her movements. The woman was making tea like she'd just asked about the weather. Connor had distinctly said he hadn't told his grandmother about the baby. How on earth could she know? The shirt Alex was wearing covered most of her belly, and she was barely beginning to show. She should have been prepared for the question, but she wasn't, and she floundered horribly.

"Mrs. Madsen…"

"Oh, dear. None of that, I hope." Johanna turned with a carton of milk in her hands. "You can call me Gram, like Connor does, or Johanna—whichever suits you best."

Alex paused. She was on shaky footing. The woman before her was shrewd, and exuded an aura of power and competence that Alex found intimidating. Yet at the same time she seemed very down to earth and without artifice. Alex couldn't read her at all, and her discomfort grew as the woman raised a questioning eyebrow at her continued silence. Somehow she had to try to gain control of the conversation, yet without seeming adversarial. She'd already argued with Connor this morning; she wasn't sure she could stand to go three rounds with his grandmother.

"Mrs. Madsen." She used the formal name as a shield. "I'm sorry. Your question took me by surprise," she finally got out.

"You *are* pregnant, aren't you?" Johanna turned her back to Alex, putting the cream and sugar on a tray with the teapot.

Alex dropped her eyes and her shoulders tensed. Never in her life had she felt more deceitful, more undeserving. Johanna had guessed about the baby—and that was sure to create problems. The best way to deal with it was head-on.

"Yes, I am. Fourteen weeks."

"And Connor says you met on Friday?" Johanna turned back, bringing the pot to the table.

Oh, didn't that sound lovely? Alex flushed. *By the way, I'm marrying your grandson. I've known him for less than a week.* She might as well march right upstairs and repack her bag. She knew how it looked, no matter what the reality was. In a cool voice she replied, "Yes. I fainted downtown and he came to my rescue."

To her surprise, a tender smile spread across Johanna's face. "Oh, my. That sounds just like Lars."

"Lars?" Alex was intrigued by the radiant look that transformed Johanna's face, making her look twenty years younger.

"My husband—Connor's grandfather."

Johanna brought the tray to the pine table while Alex hesitantly perched on a chair. They sat across the table from each other while Johanna poured the tea. Alex was wary, but found herself curious about Connor's grandfather, and what kind of man held the power to put that particular soft look on Johanna's face.

Alex wanted to believe this woman was on a friendly mission. But until she could be sure she had to be very, very careful.

"Lars was the noblest man I ever knew." Johanna chuckled a bit, on a lovely little note of remembrance. "When we met I was fifteen. I had a bicycle, you see. I'd fallen off and scraped my knee quite badly. Lars saw me by the side of the road." She smiled warmly at the memory. "His father… Connor's great-grandfather…had bought a truck for the farm the week before. Lars put my bike in the back and drove me home. He was twenty-three and, oh my, so handsome. It's where Connor gets his looks, you know." She stared at Alex knowingly over the rim of her cup.

Alex shifted in her chair. How was she to respond to that? Of course Connor was handsome. Devastatingly so. But to agree would be admitting to an attraction she didn't want, and to ignore the comment…she didn't want to be insulting, either. It would make her look like she was only after his money. She couldn't win.

"Connor is handsome. You'd be blind to miss it," she stated matter-of-factly, revealing essentially nothing.

"It's the Madsen men." Johanna nodded sagely. "There's

a picture of Lars's grandparents around somewhere, on their wedding day. He was a looker too." Johanna rose and retrieved the bag of cookies from the pantry, handing one to Alex. "It was Lars's grandfather who settled this place, you know. The government was offering homesteads. He traveled all the way from Norway to start a life here. And the farm has never left the family.

"Which is where you come in." Johanna pushed her mug aside. "I know that this isn't a regular marriage. My question is, why are you willing to marry a man you hardly know? And how much of his money do you expect to get out of the deal?"

"I beg your pardon?" Alex put down her mug, confused at the sudden turn of the conversation. First she was friendly, and now she was putting the screws on her? Alex was finding it hard to keep her balance. She understood now that it had all been a part of Johanna's strategy. Lull her into a friendly conversation and then hit her with the big guns. Alex burned inwardly with indignation. She wasn't a bad person. This whole situation wasn't as cold as it sounded.

"What's in this for you, Alexis? Because being a rancher's wife isn't the easy way out, let me assure you."

Johanna's eyes were sharp, her lips a thin, unreadable line. Alex had never seen a woman so completely put together: not a hair out of place, not a wrinkle in her clothing, even though she'd been nearly two hours in her car. Alex tucked a stray piece of hair behind her ear and tried to shake away the feeling of a chastised child. She hadn't done anything wrong or deceitful. She'd made the mistake of falling for the wrong guy once, and now she was dealing with the aftermath in the only way she knew how. She didn't deserve to be judged.

Alex dropped her cookie to the table. "I don't have any plans of being a rancher's wife. And I resent the implication that somehow I'm *extorting* money out of your grandson. I'm doing this for one reason and one only. Security for me and my baby."

For a few months she could pretend she lived in this secure, traditional world. A husband and a house, and no stress about where the next meal was coming from. It was a sham, all of it, but she had a desperate need to belong somewhere, even for such a short time. But how could she explain that to this woman? Their family tree went back several generations, right here on this farm. She would never understand how displaced and alone Alex had been for most of her life.

"When Connor met me I was alone, working as a waitress, with no real home and a baby on the way." She looked squarely into his grandmother's eyes, and gambled that Connor had outlined their agreement already.

"This all took place because he wants to save Windover, plain and simple. Connor marries me so that he can access his trust fund. After the baby is born we'll go our separate ways, and he'll help support us until I can get my feet under myself again."

She didn't use the word "divorce", even though it was the proper term. Somehow it seemed cold and hateful, even in a platonic marriage such as this. She did not look away from Johanna's serious expression. Alex didn't want to anger Johanna, but neither would she be a doormat, nor accused of being a gold-digger.

"And, to be clear, Connor approached me, not the other way around. I didn't go looking for a sugar daddy, if that's what you're implying."

"I think I already knew that." Johanna's eyes showed nothing of what she was feeling. "But I had to hear it anyway. You are doing this for your baby. What about the child's father?"

Alex winced. Ryan had been charming—too charming. Alex had fallen for him quickly, absorbing the affection and attention into her love-starved soul. But deep down she'd known he wasn't the keeper type. When she'd announced she was pregnant he had hit the door so fast she'd felt the draft. In another situation she would have said *good riddance to bad rubbish.* But this time was different. She was alone again, but with an innocent, precious baby to consider. One she was determined would have a stable, secure life.

"The biological father has no interest in parenthood, I'm afraid. He left me, and the baby I'm carrying."

Johanna rose and took her cup to the sink. Turning back, she said softly, "What do *you* ultimately want, Alexis?"

A home. Again the answer came unbidden, and it wasn't one she cared to share. This was only a temporary home and she had to remember that. What Connor had proposed would make it possible for her to build her own home, a safe, welcoming place for her child. A child who would always feel wanted and loved and a first priority. All the things her parents had tried to provide but somehow she'd missed.

"I want a good life for my baby. I want to make a home for us. I just want a place for my baby to feel loved and safe."

Johanna walked over to the table and placed a hand on Alex's shoulder. "That's a damned good answer."

Alex couldn't keep up with the changes from friend to foe to friend again, and somehow knew she was failing this test miserably.

Johanna's hand was warm on her shoulder, and Alex hadn't known how much she'd missed simple human contact. Something about Johanna's hand, firm and sure, sent feelings rushing up in Alex, and she struggled to hold them rippling beneath the surface. She couldn't remember the last time she'd even been hugged. The older woman could never understand what a simple touch could do...

"Thank you," she whispered, sweeping a few crumbs into her palm to try to escape the moment.

"How long has it been?"

Alex straightened. "Since what?"

"Oh, my dear, it's obvious," Johanna murmured, nothing but kindness softening her face. "Since someone loved you."

The tears came so quickly, so completely unexpectedly, that Alex was powerless to stop them. Johanna came forward and tucked Alex into her embrace, and she cried into the older woman's shoulder. Cried for the second time that week, when it had been years since she'd shed tears. Not once in the time she'd been alone had anyone acknowledged that she hadn't been loved. Had anyone cared that she might be lonely and afraid. But she was. She was terrified of failing. Of not being enough for her child. She was frightened, quite simply, of the unknown future.

Her breath came in halting gasps, and she desperately tried to even them out as she tasted the salt of her own tears. She had to get herself together.

Connor stepped through the front door, halting abruptly at the sight of his grandmother holding a sobbing Alex in her arms. His throat constricted at the picture they made. So much for maintaining distance. Because the sight of his fiancée and his grandmother together did something to his heart he knew he'd never get back.

Connor steered the tractor to the edge of the field and left it. Tomorrow he'd be back to continue on. Now he'd drive back to the house in the truck.

The noon meal had been tense. He'd rushed the meeting, anxious to get back early so he might arrive before Gram. But he'd been too late. When he'd entered, Alex had turned to the small bathroom off the kitchen, embarrassed, to wash her tear-streaked face and regain control. When she'd returned she had pasted on a smile and apologized that she didn't have his lunch ready. He hadn't cared less about lunch. What he'd really wanted to know was what his grandmother had done to provoke such an emotional response. He remembered Alex protesting before that she hated crying. But she'd been in the middle of a full-blown jag when he'd come in.

It was obvious his grandmother approved of Alex, no matter how unorthodox their situation.

Connor started up the pickup and shoved it into gear, a line appearing between his brows. Seeing them together that way…it had been *right* somehow.

"She's already had enough hurt in her life, that girl," Gram had warned under her breath, while Alex had been in the next room, repairing the damage to her face.

He had no plans of hurting Alex further at all. In fact, the more he saw of her, the more he knew he had to protect her. They had made a deal that benefited them both, but ultimately they were from two very different worlds. Now it was up to him to uphold his end.

He would be her friend, but there was no room for anything more. Not if he were to be fair.

As he'd left the house, Gram had said something else. "Be very careful, dear," she'd said, a hand on his arm. "I've never seen a creature more hungry for love and affection than that child."

Pulling up into the yard, he noticed Gram's car was gone. Perhaps she'd gone back to Calgary and her own apartment? Connor's stomach fluttered nervously at the thought of being alone with Alex. "Stupid fool," he chided himself as he hesitated at his own front door. If they were to be friends only, there should be nothing to be nervous about.

Alex was coming through the living room with a basket of laundry in her arms as he entered. Both stopped in surprise.

"Gram went home?"

Alex laughed, putting down the basket. "Hardly. She's put her bag in the third bedroom and dug in for the duration."

"Oh." Connor's voice registered disappointment and he put on an optimistic smile. "She'll be a great help to you."

"Oh, yes," Alex replied, a happy smile on her face. "I was terribly worried about meeting her. And we did have a few uncomfortable moments. But once she knew about the baby…"

"She knows?" He stepped forward, surprise lighting his face. All Gram had said at lunch was not to hurt Alex; she'd mentioned nothing about knowing about the pregnancy. Now here was Alex, carefree and happy. He hadn't seen that particular look on her face before, but he recognized it now. It was devoid of strain and worry. She looked like a woman who'd been given a free pass. Connor hadn't thought it possible, but it made her even more beautiful.

"Yes," she chirped. "I must have answered her questions satisfactorily. She's already making wedding plans."

Connor's head spun. The words *don't hurt her* and *hungry for love* echoed through his brain. He'd expected stiff resistance once she knew about the baby. Instead Gram had moved in?

"Is it too soon?"

"What?" he came out of his stupor and shook his head. "Oh. No, of course not, I'm surprised, that's all."

"I was too. We had a big talk this afternoon, though, Connor. Your grandmother is an amazing woman. She said she understood I didn't know much about cooking, and when I told her I'd never gardened she said I could use a helping hand. That she'd missed it, living in her condo the way she does."

"She did?"

"Uh-huh. And she said she'd help plan the wedding too."

This was getting out of hand. Weddings and gardens and babies… Connor's very logical, sensible plan was suddenly spiraling out of control. And all under the hawk-like eye of his grandmother. He agreed that she was wonderful. He also knew she was shrewd. This was her way of keeping a finger in the pie. He knew it and resented it. But he couldn't send Johanna back to Calgary. Alex was already looking forward to the help. And he was so busy with the ranch he didn't have time to spend with her except in the evenings. It wasn't fair for him to expect her to while away her days all alone. If having Johanna here made her happy, he'd keep quiet. And he'd keep his eyes wide open. Helping was one thing. Meddling, however well intentioned, was another.

Besides, the less time he spent with Alex the better. Because sooner or later he'd see her looking at him like she was right now, and he'd be stupid, and kiss her like he wanted to, and complicate *everything*.

He changed the subject.

"She gave you your first lesson in cooking, I take it?" He looked past her shoulder to the pots bubbling on the stove.

"Yes. But she said she was going into town to have supper with a friend and not to wait up."

"Probably Millie's," he surmised, naming Gram's oldest and closest friend. And if she revealed what was going on at Windover Ranch, news of his impending marriage would be common knowledge by coffee time tomorrow.

He discovered he didn't mind as much as he'd thought he would. For a moment he stared at Alex, picturing her in a long white dress, her mass of dark hair falling over her shoulders, and he couldn't breathe. Alex lifted the basket again, momentarily placing her palm on the slight bubble of her belly, and his heart contracted painfully.

Connor was as hungry for love as Alex… But he could not, would not, seek it from her. She was leaving, and the one thing he knew he could never do was abandon Windover.

CHAPTER SEVEN

"MIKE'S on his way over. He's going to run things for me today. I've gotta go into Red Deer after lunch."

Connor made the announcement as cheerfully as he could, successfully hiding his dark feeling of despair. It was nice of his friend Mike to lend a hand, but Connor was fighting a losing battle and he knew it. The source of the outbreak was still being investigated. If anything tied it to his herd he'd have to cull the whole lot. Windover would be finished. And no amount of money would save it, trust fund or not.

He picked at his pancakes, not actually eating much. If Windover was finished, he should release Alex from their agreement. Yet he wasn't ready to let go. He wasn't giving up on Windover yet, and he wasn't going to give up on her either. Sure, he could release her, but then what would she do? He'd made her a promise. And he'd deliver on it no matter what.

"We need to go shopping." Johanna interrupted the silence.

Alex and Connor looked up from their breakfast to stare at Johanna.

"I got groceries yesterday," Alex explained, her eyes darting between Johanna and Connor with confusion.

"Not that kind of shopping. Clothes shopping. You need a wedding dress, and you're already squeezing into your jeans."

Alex flushed. "I can manage," she said, spinning a piece of pancake in the syrup on her plate.

Connor nodded. "Gram's right. I'm sorry, Alex, I should have seen to it before now. But things have been…"

"Busy. It's fine."

He looked at her, dressed in the same jeans and T-shirt he was growing used to seeing. She'd asked for nothing, nothing at all. She had to have some new things. That was all there was to it. When he'd made this proposition looking after her welfare had become his duty, and he simply should have seen before now how threadbare her wardrobe was.

He looked outside at the rain falling. One of the reasons he'd decided to meet with John, Cal and Rick was that the rainy day meant no haying. He'd called them early, asking them to meet. They were ranchers, like him, who had everything to lose. And they hadn't hesitated when he'd suggested getting together.

"Why don't we go this afternoon? I can drop you off on my way, pick you up on the way back."

Alex put down her fork. "I don't want to inconvenience you, Connor."

"It's no inconvenience. In fact, I insist." He forced a grin. "Come on, I didn't think you'd fight me on a shopping trip!"

Johanna interjected. "A bride needs a suitable dress, and maternity clothes will soon be a must. We're going to need a whole day, dear."

Connor met his grandmother's gaze, relieved. He'd been thinking that Alex had no wedding dress. She had no more than what she'd brought in that single bag. Yet he hadn't known how to go about saying it without hurting Alex's feelings. Coming from Johanna, it seemed less critical than he'd imagined.

"We can go this morning."

"Really, you two, this isn't necessary…" Alex interjected, pushing her plate away.

"Nonsense. Connor, there's no reason why you can't join

us for the morning, have lunch, and drop us off after at the formal wear store to shop for dresses." She winked at him. "We *will* spare you the wedding dress shopping."

A morning shopping wasn't normally what he'd call fun, but when he looked at Alex he saw reluctance mingled with a tiny bit of anticipation. When was the last time someone had treated her to a shopping spree? When was the last time he'd taken a day off?

"I'm game if you are, Alex."

Alex had never had anyone treat her to a day of shopping, and the sheer novelty of it was exciting. Yet she hesitated to agree. She didn't have any money of her own, and felt like enough of a freeloader already, without Connor and Johanna paying for an entirely new wardrobe.

"I'm sure Connor would like to see you in something other than jeans and T-shirts," Johanna went on, aiming a pointed glare in Connor's direction.

Alex met Connor's eyes. There was nothing in the warm depths that criticized her appearance. In fact they crinkled at the corners a bit, giving her a strange sense of reassurance. She couldn't read what he was thinking, but his face was relaxed and amiable as he responded, "You deserve it."

She certainly didn't feel like she deserved it, and she was so used to looking after herself that she wasn't comfortable with someone else footing the bill. She certainly didn't want Connor to feel as if she were taking advantage of his generosity, or his grandmother's either, for that matter.

"It's settled, then." Johanna resumed eating, bringing Alex's misgivings to a screeching halt. "We can take my car, Connor. It'll be much easier than the truck."

Alex got the sneaky feeling she was being railroaded, but knew it would be fruitless to argue. Besides, if she didn't get some new clothes soon she'd be running around with her pants unbuttoned. Practicality warred with guilt, and practicality won.

"I'll get ready," she answered faintly, still not convinced it was a good idea.

The first place they hit was a shopping mall, arriving just as the stores were pushing back their metal and glass doors.

"You need maternity clothes," Johanna insisted, and led a reluctant Alex inside by the hand. The first customers of the day, they got the saleslady's undivided attention.

"Only the basics," Alex insisted, looking at Connor. He hung back, and she wondered why in the world he'd agreed to come along. Surely he didn't consider this "fun"? As Johanna fluttered around, she wondered what exactly Connor *did* think constituted fun. She didn't even know that much about him, yet here she was planning their wedding and shopping for clothes. Clothes *he* was going to pay for.

She didn't want to be accused of taking more than she needed. She looked around at the racks of clothing, amazed at how stylish and cute they were. She picked up a black crepe top, with ties to the back and tiny pink flowers dotted over it. In a very few short months her tummy would be rounded and full. She touched the warm area where right now her baby lay. Motherhood. Somehow, shopping for maternity wear drove home the fact that she was going to be a mother more than anything else had—even the crazy deal with Connor. Someday in the near future she was going to have a tiny bundle to love, to nurture, to care for.

"Are you OK?" Connor touched Alex's shoulder.

Alex half turned, letting out a breathless laugh. "It just hit me. I'm going to be a mother."

Connor smiled. "You started to turn pale." He scanned the racks, and shook his head at the sight of his grandmother chatting animatedly with the clerk. "So—excited, or scared to death?"

She couldn't help it, she laughed, suddenly very glad he'd come along. "A little of both?"

She had an ally in Connor, although she had no idea why she deserved it. Johanna held up a hand, waggling it in the air and rattling hangers.

"I think I'm being summoned." She aimed a wry smile at him, gratified to see his own mirror hers.

"I predict you'll be a while, from that gleam in her eye. I've seen it before. I'll go find us some coffee."

"That sounds good," she answered, unable to draw her eyes away from his. It was silly to be here, gazing into each other's eyes, but somehow they'd locked and clung until her heart grew heavy in her chest.

His eyes shifted to over her shoulder.

"Here. Try these on. I thought you'd be happier with casual." Johanna interrupted the moment and Connor quietly left. In some strange way she felt better when he was by her side, but she certainly didn't expect him to hang around a maternity shop and comment on fit and style.

Alex was led away, then ensconced in a changing room, handing clothes in and out as she tried on several outfits. In the end she agreed to two pairs of jeans, two pairs of summer shorts, several casual cotton shirts, a sweet pajama set in white with lace trim, and a good outfit for special occasions—a black skirt with a ruffled hem, paired with a scooped-neck floral top.

"It's too much." She put a hand over the top of Johanna's left as the older woman signed the credit card slip.

"Nonsense. Alex, you need these things. It's a pleasure to provide them for you. I always only ever had a son and grandsons to buy for, and boys are too practical. It's a treat for me just to be able to buy something pink and feminine. Indulge me."

Alex took two of the bags in her hands. "And I thank you. But…I'm used to providing for myself."

"You're working hard to learn up at Windover. You are

trying to be what Connor needs right now. That's payment enough for me. I know Connor agrees."

She was what Connor needed? A screw-up in the kitchen? A stranger who knew nothing about ranching? As far as she was concerned, she'd been on the receiving end of all the benefit and hadn't given much in return. Now Johanna was treating her like a real granddaughter. The girl longing for a home was irresistibly attracted to that, while the practical woman inside knew that it would only hurt more in the end when she had to leave.

Johanna took the remainder of the bags, nudging her out the door. "Come on. You need shoes."

Connor had been waiting outside and now handed her a paper cup, the tab folded back already and the letters "dec" printed roughly on the top. He'd thought to get her decaf, she realized as Johanna herded them on to the shoe store. His consideration was a constant surprise.

Feeling somewhat helpless, she watched as Connor waited patiently on a bench outside the store while she bought casual shoes, a pair of black patent slingbacks for dressy, and white satin slippers for the wedding.

By lunchtime, their arms were laden with bags. In addition to the footwear and maternity clothes, she'd purchased new socks and underwear at the department store. She'd also taken some of her own money, what little there was of it, and bought Connor a pair of new T-shirts. The one he'd had on first thing this morning was worn around the collar. She couldn't think of anything else appropriate to buy, but she was determined not to go home with nothing for him. She hadn't ever bought a man clothing before, and without knowing sizes was a fish out of water. Socks were too impersonal, and underwear…far too intimate. But T-shirts she could manage without too much trouble. Besides, it would be a treat to see his wide chest in them, the way the sleeves outlined the dip in his triceps…

"I'm famished. Let's have lunch." Johanna led Alex down the hall to the restaurant housed on the corner.

Alex waited while Connor requested a table, then put a hand on his arm when Johanna excused herself to go to the ladies' room. "Lunch is on me. Please."

She'd accepted enough today. She didn't have much, but she had enough of her own money left after the T-shirts that she could at least buy lunch.

"You don't have to do that." He took a seat in the booth opposite her.

"But I want to. I'm not used to…to charity." Guilt and shame trickled through her simply from saying the word.

"You're not charity. I'm getting something out of this deal too, remember?" He reached over and put his hand on top of hers. "You're helping me, Alex. Right now it's safe to say you're all the hope I've got."

His thumb was tracing circles over the side of her hand and she didn't think he was even aware he was doing it. Let alone realizing what the simple touch was doing to her insides.

She swallowed. "Then indulge me. You've done so much for me already. Let me buy you lunch."

He hesitated a moment, but relented. "Deal. But I'll warn you. Watching you shop works up my appetite."

Alex laughed as a waitress brought tall glasses of iced water. "Now that the sickness seems to be getting better, I could eat all the time."

His thumb kept circling. "You know, Alex, I can't believe I didn't think of this before now. It's not right that you have to come to me for every penny. There are things you're going to need—for yourself, for the house, getting ready for the baby. I'll make sure I get you a checkbook and a debit card. I'm sorry I didn't look after it before."

He was going to trust her with his bank account? Alex tried

not to gape and instead grabbed her water and sipped, hiding her shocked face.

His thumb stopped and he squeezed her hand. "Did I say something wrong?"

"No, no, not at all," she stammered, then cleared her throat as it seemed to suddenly become hoarse. "I'm just surprised, that's all."

"Is there a reason I shouldn't trust you?"

"No!" She finally lifted her eyes and saw he was watching her steadily. Like he already knew the answer. "Of course not. It's just…"

How could she explain what such a practical, simple act meant to her? That he trusted her to such an extent that she could use his money without asking? That it was one more thing binding her to him and giving her this uncanny sense of normalcy in an otherwise unorthodox arrangement?

"It makes sense, that's all. I've taken you away from your income…I agreed to provide for you. That doesn't mean you don't get some say in the matter."

"It's more than I expected. You and your grandmother— you've been far too generous with me. She paid for *everything* this morning. I'm not used to that."

Connor took a sip of his water, pulling his hand away from hers. "Don't you feel one bit of guilt. Gram is having a ball. She hasn't done this since…well, in many years. But she and Mom used to do it all the time."

"They were close?" Alex prodded gently.

Connor nodded. "Yes, they were. Gram always said, 'Melissa, you're my best daughter.' I think she always wanted a little girl of her own, but there was only Dad. She and Mom were peas in a pod. I think she was a little disappointed that one of us wasn't a girl and she didn't get a granddaughter to spoil."

She smiled at the fond tone of remembrance in his voice. It was good he remembered the good times. She wished she could, but somehow all she seemed to feel was regret and a sense of being cheated out of something.

"Mom and Gram used to take little trips like this all the time…sometimes even for something as silly as buying school supplies for Jim and me. But they always had fun. Dad always said it was an excuse for them to get away from the farm for a day and treat themselves."

"So that's why you came today?"

He looked up and saw Johanna approaching. "I thought you could both use a little of that."

She couldn't believe she hadn't considered it before. When Connor had lost his parents, Johanna had lost a son, daughter-in-law, and grandson. That pain had to be with her still.

"Have we ordered yet?"

"Just waiting for you." Connor scooched over and made room for Johanna to sit.

"Whew. I worked up an appetite this morning. Haven't had this much fun since—"

When she broke off, Alex looked up at Connor and was happy he'd told her what he had.

"Connor was just telling me about his mother. And how you used to sneak off for day trips like this."

"Oh, we did. We always came back with more than we went for, but we had a ball. You're a lot like her, you know."

"I am?" Alex put down her menu and her eyebrows lifted with surprise. "I wouldn't think so."

Johanna laughed, the rusty sound that always made Alex smile. "Oh, yes. The dark hair, pretty eyes. But more than that, you're strong. Stubborn, too, I can tell. And you have a big heart, Alex. I saw that right off. Don't you think so, Connor?"

Alex dropped her eyes, both at the unexpected praise and the blatant attempt at matchmaking. Did Connor see that in her too? How could he, when she couldn't see it in herself?

He covered the awkward moment with a laugh. "I certainly

agree with the stubborn thing," he joked, then related the tale of her first cooked meal, and how determined she was to conquer the kitchen. "If supper last night was any indication, your stubborn streak will serve you well. The ham was delicious."

Alex accepted the compliment graciously, but wondered, as the server took their orders, if he did think she was much like his mother and if that was a good or a bad thing. His long leg bumped hers beneath the table and her stomach twisted. How were they supposed to come through this unscathed and unchanged? She was already feeling like a real part of this family, being included and welcomed…and the wedding hadn't even happened yet.

Johanna changed the subject, asking about wedding details, and they got so occupied with the topic that Alex quite forgot her misgivings until later.

After lunch they left the mall, and after a few quick turns Connor parked in front of a small strip-mall, gave them his return time, and Alex found herself entering a formal wear store. Mannequins dressed in white gowns stood in one window, one with a tuxedoed man on her arm. Inside were two solid rooms of formal wear. She took off her shoes, gripped her purse nervously, and followed Johanna into the reception area.

"May I help you?" A young woman, dressed in the latest fashion, looked up from the appointment book behind her desk.

"Yes. Johanna Madsen, and this is Alexis Grayson. We're shopping for a wedding dress today."

"Congratulations!" The woman smiled. "Come right in."

Alex was silent as Jennifer, as it stated on her name tag, and Johanna hashed over what sort of style would suit her. Never in her life had she shopped in such a place! All around her were dresses in white and cream satin, some adorned with lace, others with intricate beading and crystals.

A bride.

But not a bride. An impostor. This wasn't a real marriage,

and to pretend it was, was sacrilege. She didn't deserve a fancy white dress with all the trimmings.

She pulled on Johanna's arm. Johanna sent Jennifer an apologetic look.

"Excuse us a moment."

"I can't do this." Alex looked at Johanna evenly. "It isn't right. We both know this isn't a real marriage. It feels wrong to put on this big show when we both know that in a few months it'll be over. Let's just go somewhere else and pick out a nice dress and it'll do. Please. This is all…too much."

Johanna must have taken pity on her, because she acquiesced. "All right. But, Alex, people are going to wonder if you show up at your wedding in an everyday dress. You should at least have a proper dress. Connor's friends…his neighbors…will expect it."

She was engaged in a losing battle and she knew it. Not only that, but there was a small part of her that wanted to do him proud, to show up on their wedding day looking the way a bride should look. To see that gleam of appreciation in his eyes, even if it wasn't for real.

"Oh, all right. But nothing over the top."

Johanna found the sales clerk again, and before Alex could say *Here comes the bride* she found herself again in a changing room, three separate dresses hanging before her.

The first two didn't seem quite right, but the third time was the charm. Alex emerged from the change area smiling. "I like this one."

Standing before the full-length mirror, she fell in love with it.

Strapless, the satin bodice was short, gathered in an empire style just beneath her breasts, with a thin stripe of satin ribbon marking the seam and the top of the bustline above. Beneath, it flowed gracefully to the floor, a filmy overskirt of organza adding romance to the look. It was simple and stunning. She pressed a hand to her belly. Even if she started to show more in the next few weeks, the empire waist and overskirt would camouflage things perfectly.

"I'm going to get your shoes," Johanna murmured, her voice tinged with emotion. "It's beautiful, Alex," she added, before disappearing to the car to retrieve their earlier purchase.

The slippers slid on, and Alex knew that this was the one. "I love it."

She checked the price tag and almost choked.

"I can't let you do this," she protested to Johanna, but it was to no avail.

"You can and you will," the old lady returned decisively. "I promise you, you will not regret it, Alexis."

Jennifer spoke up. "It doesn't need a bit of altering. Amazing, really. We can have one ordered in for you within eight weeks."

"This wedding is happening a week from Saturday," Johanna said coolly, while Alex was still stupefied by the eight-week ordering time. "Go get changed," she ordered Alex. "I'll look after everything."

Thirty minutes later they were in the car, heading west, the trunk loaded with maternity clothes and the back seat holding one very new, very extravagant dress, and one very nervous bride-to-be.

Connor was a smart man. And he knew better than to ask what in the world was in the garment bag that Alex had carried from the car and into the house. Alex was looking relaxed and happy, and even seemed a little excited as she scooted up the stairs with her wedding finery, presumably so that he wouldn't see. It was endearing, really, despite the odd situation they'd put themselves in.

And for some reason Alex and Gram seemed to get on like a house on fire. Mealtimes were fun now, with easy banter and the two of them ganging up on him about wedding details. Honestly, he didn't care. All he wanted was a small, nice ceremony. Something intimate and simple. The details he was more than happy to leave to the women.

Summer days were long, and it was a good thing, because he was so busy it kept him from thinking too much. Besides haying and the feed crops and looking after livestock, there were many more phone calls and e-mails lately, all dealing with the crisis. The U.S. borders were closed indefinitely to all Canadian beef—and other markets were following suit. Something, *something* had to happen soon. With every bill paid, the balance in the bank account got lower and lower. After his meeting he was no further ahead. Everything was at a standstill. Everyone was waiting for the verdict on the source of the disease. Everyone he knew was praying that their herd wouldn't have to be slaughtered. And all the while the money he did receive domestically was a drop in the bucket compared to what he needed.

The one time he relaxed was in the evenings, coming in to Alex's and Gram's company. Their happy chatter and laughter lightened his load more than he wanted to admit.

Two days after the shopping trip, he escaped to the den to work on the computer. Grace Lundquist had been by with the account book, and it didn't look good. He sighed, rubbing his temples as he rested his elbows on the desk. He wished he could put it aside and maybe watch some television with Alex and Gram. Resolutely he set his jaw. There had to be a way to work the numbers. He went over the columns again, wondering where he could save and what absolutely needed to be spent.

"Long day?"

Alex's voice interrupted him, and he couldn't help the warmth that spread through him with just a few words from her lips. "The longest."

"Can I come in?"

He swiveled in his chair, turned to see her hesitating in the doorway, her form backlit by the light from the kitchen. "Of course you can."

She offered a small smile, stepped lightly inside. "I forgot to give you something the other day. It's not much, but…"

She held out the bag containing the shirts. "I thought you could use a new supply."

He took the bag from her hands, peering inside. "T-shirts." He looked up, a smile smoothing the lines of worry from his face. "You didn't have to do that."

She sighed. "I couldn't spend the whole day shopping and not bring something home for you. I only wish I could have…well, never mind."

"They're great. I appreciate the thought as much as the gift, Alex." It had been many years since anyone had thought to give him a present "just because."

Her eyes slid to the computer screen and the open books on the desk. "It's bad, isn't it, Connor? I can tell by the stress written all over your face."

He didn't even attempt to hide it as wrinkles marred his brow. "It's bad. The whole industry is crumpling around us."

"Will we make it? Won't your trust fund money help?"

His throat grew so dry it hurt. She had said "we", not "you". He wasn't sure if it helped knowing she was in it with him or not.

His ancestors had started with nothing and made this place work. His great-grandfather had persevered throughout the Depression when other farmers had abandoned their land, looking for work. It damn near killed him to admit, "I don't know. It'll help for a while, but I don't know."

She nodded, but he saw the flicker of uncertainty on her face. "Alex, no matter what happens with Windover, I made you a promise. I said I would help provide for you and your baby, and I will."

"You always keep your promises, don't you? Don't worry

about the baby and me. We're all in this together." She came even closer, close enough that he had to lift his chin to look in her eyes, see the faint flush on her cheeks.

She smiled down at him, her face soft with understanding. "If it'll help, we can just have a Justice of the Peace here for the wedding. I don't need all the trappings that Johanna seems determined to have."

There was no way he was going to deprive her of a nice wedding. Not after all she was willing to go through to make this whole plan work. "It's not that much when you look at the big picture," he conceded. "A small, intimate affair is no problem. And secretly…" he smiled up at her "…I think Gram is having a marvelous time."

She leaned back against the desk, resting her hips there. He saw the pouch forming at her waist and wondered at the tiny life growing inside her. When he looked up and met her eyes again, she was smiling. It was a smile of contentment, of happiness, of peace.

"He's growing."

"I noticed." He realized she had called the baby "he" and wondered if she had some maternal instinct that told her it was a boy.

"Each day I feel stronger. Each day," she said softly, "I know I'm happy I'm going to be a mother. That's not something I expected. That's something I can thank you for."

"Me?" How in the world was he possibly responsible for that?

"I had no idea what I was going to do when I found out I was pregnant. When Ryan left me I…well, I certainly knew I was on my own. But you…being here…it's given me something. I don't know if it's Windover, or the open space, or the kindness you and your grandmother have shown me…" She shrugged. "But I'm not afraid now. I don't feel alone. Thank you for that."

Instead of making him feel better, he felt the weight of increased responsibility. For several years now his whole life had been responsibility—running Windover single-handedly, finding a way to keep it. Now he was responsible for this slip of a girl, one who'd been hurt as much as he, and her unborn child.

"You look so tired," she whispered, and her finger moved of its own accord, tracing along the edge of his face, tucking some errant hair over his ear. "Why do you put so much on yourself?"

"Because there's no one else," he replied, his voice weary and worn.

She tilted up his chin. "Not any more. Let me help you, Connor, like you help me."

He reached down and touched her hand, gripping her fingers and pulling her down until she sat on his lap, while the chair leaned back with a resonant creak. Her hands fell instinctively over his shoulders, and wordlessly he looped his hands around her hips, holding her close.

She was warm, comforting, solid. Someone he could lean on and not fall. Her heart beat steadily against his shoulder and he pulled her closer. "Just this," he whispered and, somehow knowing exactly what he needed, she lifted her knees until she was snuggled in his arms.

And they sat that way in the twilight, until the sun disappeared behind the mountains and the moon rose over the prairie.

CHAPTER EIGHT

CONNOR stood in the centre of the dressing room at a formal wear shop in Red Deer, rolling his eyes as the salesman fluttered around, checking seams and hems. This had been his grandmother's idea. He had thought he'd wear one of the two suits hanging in his closet. But, no, Gram had insisted he buy a new one. At least she wasn't asking him to rent a tuxedo. The plain black suit was well cut and of fine material. The shirt he wore was snowy white and stiff, contrasting with the light blue silk tie. It was more than he was used to, but he had to admit it looked nice.

He had considered resisting, but then he'd thought of Alex and her wedding dress in the plastic garment bag in her closet. He remembered how she'd sat on his lap, saying nothing, just being there for him, and he knew he would do it for her. For Connor, the week before the wedding had passed in a blur. Between working, the stress of dealing with the industry crisis, and wedding plans, he'd hardly had a moment to call his own. He should have been preoccupied with thoughts of the ranch, but instead all he'd been able to think about was marrying Alex.

He'd asked her for a paper marriage. Certainly he couldn't show her that his feelings were changing. Thankfully, he hadn't had any moments to share with Alex this week. After their intimate scene the other night, it was far better to keep some distance between them. Especially since it was the very last thing he wanted. But what would happen after Gram left, and the two of them were left alone at Windover? He couldn't avoid her forever. And being near her…did something to him so unexpected and astonishing that he wanted to run *from* it as much as he wanted to run *to* it.

He removed his jacket and handed it back to the salesman. He'd have to be very careful. They hadn't discussed any sort of time frame, yet he knew that when the baby was born and she was on her feet she'd want to be on her own, to start her own life—one that didn't include him. That was the arrangement they'd made, and he'd honor it.

He'd passed by the baby keepsakes in the jewelry store yesterday, wanting to buy a gift for her child yet knowing it would be a mistake. In the end he'd walked away from the silver money banks and cups. It was not his place to do such a thing, and no matter how his heart longed to, he knew it was impossible.

He had to guard his heart. Because she could have it all too easily.

When he stepped into the house, his errand finished and the garment bag in his hand, everything was quiet and still. "Alex?" His voice echoed through. Knitting his brows, he hung his suit over a doorknob and went in search of her.

He found them, together, in the garden in the mid-afternoon sun, their heads shaded from the sun. Gram wore her wide-brimmed straw hat, and Alex had taken one of his battered ball caps from the hook and pulled her dark ponytail through the back.

For a while he indulged himself and watched. They were laughing and chatting, Gram's knees resting on a green foam pad and Alex, more flexible, squatting beside a row of peas, pulling out weeds and depositing them in a metal bucket. Gram said something under her breath, and Alex's lilting laughter floated across the air to him. He smiled in response to the happy sound.

When he'd brought her here, she hadn't known a pea plant from a dandelion.

Alex reached for a weed, a little too far, lost her balance, and landed on her rump in the dirt.

Johanna lifted her head, tilted back her hat, and laughed heartily. He couldn't help but join in, and Alex swiveled her head to the sound.

He was chuckling, and she turned a brilliant shade of red that had nothing to do with hours in the sun.

"Sitting down on the job, Alex?" His long legs stepped over the rows of vegetables until he stood before her, offering his hand. "Gram won't give you a break? She always was a slave driver."

Alex took his hand. It was warm and rough, and her face flamed more at the touch. Since that night in the study she'd been careful to keep her hands to herself. And perhaps it was silly to get worked up over a little bit of contact. But each time he touched her it was easier to imagine things weren't as platonic as they seemed. She withdrew her fingers slowly, savoring the touch. It was all she would allow herself. It wouldn't do for her to get fanciful ideas only to have it ruin the tentative friendship they'd forged. Friends were hard to come by, and she'd had precious few over the years.

"Perhaps some lemonade's in order." Johanna's voice intruded. "I'll go in and whip some up."

Alex pulled her hand from Connor's and tried to smile at Johanna. "Let me help you."

"Alex, wait." Connor's voice stopped her. "Gram, we'll meet you inside in a minute." He turned back to Alex. "There's something I want to show you first."

He took her hand and led her around the side of the house towards the east lawn, where the ceremony was to be held. She followed, brushing her free hand against her leg to try and rid it of the garden dirt. "I hope the weather holds for Saturday," she tried cheerfully, knowing she sounded overly chatty but unable to stop the nervous quiver in her voice. "If it rains, I suppose we'll have to move everything inside."

"That would be a shame," he rejoined smoothly, and her feet stopped abruptly at the sight that greeted her.

"You…did you…make this yourself?"

She stared at a pristine white arch, perfectly curved and accented with fine half-inch lattice. She'd thought the only canopy they'd have on Saturday would be the fluttering leaves on the poplar tree, but this would add a special touch.

"I did."

"When did you find the time?" She pulled her hand from his, all eyes for the fine craftsmanship. Her fingers ran down the side, imagining it twined with ivy and a few roses here and there. "Oh, it's beautiful, Connor. Simply beautiful."

She turned back to him, gratified to see him smiling widely at her.

"You really like it? I wasn't sure it would fit in with your plans. This wedding stuff is a little out of my league. My brain shuts off when I hear the words 'floral arrangements' and 'table linens'."

"Fit in? It's perfect. Is this why you were spending all your evenings in the barn? I thought you were working with the livestock."

He raised his hands. "Guilty as charged."

She circled it, smoothing it with her hand, making it almost a caress. "I've always wanted one, but I figured the cost to rent one was too much, so I never even mentioned it."

Her voice trailed away. "I'll shut up now," she whispered, blushing while he stuck his hands in his pockets and laughed.

"You're welcome. I'm glad you like it."

"I do. It's perfect." *Like you,* she thought suddenly. He was nearly perfect. The perfect gentleman, solicitous and caring, generous and understanding. Hardworking and modest, and willing to accept her and her unborn child without judgement.

He stared at his feet suddenly. "I know Saturday isn't a regular wedding day, but…"

"I know what you meant by the thought, Connor." She smiled, a little ray of shy intimacy. "It's a romantic notion for a rancher, you know. And I appreciate it more than I can say."

Against her better judgement she went to stand before him and laid a hand on his forearm. "It's not wrong to have wishes, to pretend that this is something that it isn't. If we just went through with it, no fuss, no muss, it'd be cold…I'm glad you're not that type of person. It means a lot, knowing you want it to be special in some way. Even if it's not the real way." Even as she said it she felt wishes of her own start to rise up, and she pushed them down, struggling to remain practical.

His hand slid out of his pocket, folding her palm in his as his dark eyes plumbed her lighter blue ones. For a long moment he seemed to search for words, finding none.

Alex squeezed his hand, longing to stand on tiptoe and reassure him with a kiss, knowing she could not. The moment dragged on until she could hardly bear it.

"Gram probably has that lemonade ready," he murmured roughly. "We should go in." He touched a finger to her nose. "You're getting sunburn, and I'm sure you don't want to walk down the aisle with a red nose."

She put a testing hand up to her face. "You're right. Let's go in."

He led the way, and all the while Alex felt like she was getting in far deeper than was prudent.

"I got my suit today," he said, taking a seat at the table

and stretching out his legs. "Another thing you can check off your list."

"That's good. Because you've got two days before the wedding and everything is pretty much done." Johanna put a pitcher of pale yellow liquid in the middle of the table while Alex took out three glasses.

"Johanna's taken care of everything," she said, placing a tumbler before him. "Things are all set for Saturday. I could never have done it alone."

Doing it alone probably would have consisted of a Justice of the Peace in the living room, but watching Alex blossom under his grandmother's attention had been rewarding. She was more open, smiled more. There was a warmth that had been missing before that now radiated from her. Gram had been right. Alex *had* been hungry for love. The way she was appreciative of everything, how she seemed to understand the meaning behind the smallest gesture, made him realize she took nothing for granted. It saddened him that her life had been difficult, yet it was singularly the strongest thing that drew him to her.

She certainly did not deserve to be hurt again, and he'd make sure that their relationship stayed in a place where they could always be friends. If his wedding promises meant nothing else, they would mean that.

In forty-eight hours, she'd be Mrs. Alexis Madsen. The minister would pronounce them husband and wife and he'd kiss her and they'd cut the cake and…

And he'd kiss her.

Dear Lord, he hadn't thought of that. His hand swiped over his mouth. Kissing Alex, in front of witnesses. If holding her hand caused her to blush, what would a kiss do? Would she sense his hesitation, or wonder at his motives? Could he satisfy himself with one kiss?

Connor pushed his chair away hastily, rising and putting his glass in the sink. "Thanks for the lemonade. I've gotta go."

Alex stared after Connor with wide eyes, hearing the screen door slap into the frame with a bang.

"What got into him?"

Johanna laughed, eyes twinkling. "I think he's realized he's getting married in two days."

Alex's eyes stared at the door as if she could see him on the other side of it, hurrying to the barn. "Two days," she whispered, desperate to quiet her churning nerves at the thought. In two days they would stand before his family and friends and make promises they didn't intend to keep.

Alex swallowed the lump in her throat, watching him cross the yard with long strides. Before that happened Alex knew they had to talk. Because there were promises, real ones, that needed to be made before they proceeded with this sham of a marriage.

The portable arch was in place beneath the huge old poplar, and the white folding chairs, numbering only twenty-four, were in small, precise rows. Several feet away, over by the deck, was a dance floor, large and roughly constructed of plywood by an obliging neighbor. Leaned up against the deck were four long, foldable tables that tomorrow would be adorned with white tablecloths, all borrowed from the church. Inside the house, small cakes and sweets were in boxes in the freezer. Millie, Johanna's longtime friend, was providing the wedding feast. On one hand Alex was touched by the willingness of the Madsens' friends to help, yet on the other it only increased the pressure she felt, knowing she would be Mrs. Connor Madsen in name only.

Alex surveyed the backyard, her hands twisting nervously. She wasn't entirely sure Connor was going to go through with it. Ever since yesterday afternoon he'd made darn sure he'd kept his distance, only appearing when absolutely necessary. If he were having second thoughts, she wished he'd come and say so, put her out of her misery. One minute she was nervous as sin about the ceremony, and the next she was petrified she'd have to send the guests home due to lack of a groom.

Today he'd escaped early to the fields, only coming in for meals. The minister had arrived at five sharp, and Connor had rushed in from the barn to hastily go over the details of the ceremony tomorrow. But he'd been distracted, fidgeting like he wanted to be anywhere else. And who could blame him? She wasn't the world's greatest catch, now, was she? Granted, she'd improved, thanks to Johanna's help. She was learning about gardening and her cooking was getting better. She was for the first time putting down some roots, just like the fragile green plants sprouting in the garden.

Roots that were going to make it even harder to leave when the time came. But the fact remained she was pregnant with another man's baby. And even if she wanted to help Connor financially, her earning potential was severely limited. She'd never gone to school beyond twelfth grade. She knew in her head that this was only for a few months, but her heart was constantly disagreeing with her, picturing much, much more.

A real marriage. A real husband and a real home and a real family.

She laughed to herself. Well, if that wasn't putting the cart before the horse. This whole situation was so unorthodox she could do nothing more than shake her head at her turbulent feelings and hope for the best.

"You're looking glum."

Johanna's voice intruded behind her and she jumped, startled. "Sorry."

"Second thoughts?"

She turned to the older lady, seeing understanding on her face. "It's just…so close, you know?"

"You'll do fine. You've got backbone. You know what's right."

"But is this right?" she implored Johanna with her hands

outstretched. "Is this fair to Connor? A temporary wife carrying someone else's baby? I got so wrapped up in the fun of planning tomorrow that I forgot what it's supposed to be about…and what it's really about."

Johanna's eyes softened, a glimmer of a smile tipping the corners of her mouth. "Oh, my dear," she murmured, putting a hand on Alex's hair. "Don't sell yourself short."

Alex swallowed. "But Connor…"

"Is upstairs in the shower, and hungry to boot. I'm off to Millie's to look after some last-minute arrangements."

So she and Connor would have time alone after all. Alex didn't know whether to be grateful or petrified.

When Connor came downstairs, Alex had fixed him a plate. He was clean-shaven, his hair brushed back and glistening with water from his shower. She recognized the fresh smell of his deodorant and the slightly spicy scent of his shampoo, and her stomach clenched.

"I'll get your chicken off the grill," she explained, hurrying outside to the barbeque to retrieve his chicken breast. He sat down quietly as she placed the plate before him, heaped with mixed greens, chicken, and macaroni salad.

"Gram made this before she left?" he asked, putting some of the salad in his mouth.

"No, I did."

His eyes met hers, and she sensed warmth in them for the first time in the past forty-eight hours.

"It tastes like hers. Exactly."

Alex smiled. "Well, I did tell you I was a good student."

"Aren't you eating?" He gestured to the place across from him with his fork.

"I ate earlier."

"I see."

Alex made herself busy around the kitchen while Connor finished his meal, and then, clearing his plate, she took a breath. She had to be a grownup and do this. And do it now before she lost her nerve.

"I think we should talk."

He stilled, wary, and Alex's nerves twisted and turned as everything she'd planned to say went rushing out of her head completely.

"Talk about what?"

She put his dishes in the dishwasher, keeping her back towards him. *Coward,* she grumbled to herself. She had to do this. She was an adult. Difficult conversations had to be faced.

"About us. About what's going to happen tomorrow."

"I see."

She turned, facing him, but his expression was flat and completely closed off, and she wasn't sure how to proceed. "Please, Connor. I can't pretend that tomorrow is what it will look like."

"I can't either."

His words left her feeling strangely empty. She shouldn't want him to mean his vows, but somehow she did. It was wrong, and misguided, but she would admit only to herself that she had feelings for Connor. Deep feelings. Feelings he surely didn't reciprocate, so she'd do the right thing here.

"Our vows tomorrow…they're the forever kind." She sat in the chair next to him, resting her hands in her lap, the backs pressed together between her knees. "We both know that forever isn't what this is about." *No matter what my traitorous heart is saying right at this moment.* "But I think we should make promises. To each other, tonight, about what we can expect over the next several months."

"You mean temporary vows?"

"Yes," she breathed with relief, glad he understood what she was getting at.

He sighed, and she resisted the urge to reach up and tuck that errant piece of hair behind his ear, the one that always seemed determined to curl. His eyes searched her face, and she knew that she would never be able to resist him when he looked at her that way.

"This means a lot to you, doesn't it?"

She nodded. "Tomorrow…we'll just be making empty promises. I'm not comfortable with that. Because there are things I want to promise you. Truly."

Trembling, she reached out and took his workworn hand in hers. "I promise you, Connor, that for the time we're married I will do all I can to make your life easier, not harder. I'll try my best to look after the beautiful home you've entrusted me with, and—" she smiled faintly "—I'll try not to poison you with my bad cooking. I'll be a friend to you, and a comfort, if you'll let me. I'll help you in any way I can. You've only to ask. Those are the promises I can make to you."

Oh, his eyes. So warm, with compassion and understanding and with an edge of something she didn't quite comprehend. He covered her hand with his own and squeezed. "I have promises to make to you, too," he said softly. "Look at me, Alex," he commanded, when she dropped her eyes.

She met his gaze and was caught, unable to look away.

"I promise, Alex, to provide for you, and the baby you're carrying, for as long as you need. I promise to share my home with you, so that it's your home too, because you've been without one for so long. I promise that I won't be the one to hurt you, not when you've been hurt already. I will be *your* friend and *your* comfort, if you'll let me." His voice dropped, an intimate whisper as he repeated her own words back to her. "I'll help you in any way I can. You've only to ask. Those are the promises I can make to you."

Her eyes filled, shining with unshed tears at his words. He meant them. She knew it. And for her they were more romantic than any flowery vows from a book could ever be. Somehow this handsome man—still so much a stranger—

knew exactly what she needed and was willing to give it to her, wholeheartedly, unreservedly.

In that shining moment she knew another truth that would make tomorrow even harder.

She was falling in love with Connor Madsen.

"Alex? Are you OK?"

Her eyes had closed against the brief shaft of bittersweet pain that pierced her as she realized the one man she couldn't have was the one she was falling head over heels in love with. Swallowing, she pushed back her chair and broke their hand clasp. "I'm fine. I'm just tired," she explained, avoiding the skeptical look that raised his eyebrows with doubt. "I think I'll get ready for bed. There's a lot to do tomorrow."

She avoided looking at him, knowing her abrupt change of mood had to be confusing.

"Mike's looking after the chores tomorrow. There's no need for either of us to get up at daybreak," he offered. "You should sleep in. Get your beauty rest."

"Thanks. For…for everything. Goodnight, Connor."

She fled before he saw the tears that glistened on her cheeks.

CHAPTER NINE

THE wedding day dawned clear, with a light blue sky sparsely dotted with fluffy white clouds. Alex woke at six. She'd retired early the night before but, instead of taking advantage, she knew she had to get up and help Johanna get things ready before she dressed in her gown.

Quietly she slipped from her room and down the hall to the bathroom. She wanted to avoid Connor at all costs this morning. It had nothing to do with it being bad luck to see the bride, but more about keeping a level head. It would be all too easy to let the romance of the day sweep her away. What she needed to do was make sure everything was in readiness for the guests. Make it seem real. She ran hot water and washed her face and brushed her teeth before tiptoeing back to her room to get dressed.

Connor heard her shuffling about. He'd been awake since four, but had stayed beneath the sheets, thinking. It had nothing to do with habit and everything to do with getting married today. Getting married to Alex.

He remembered the promises she'd made him. She tried hard, he could see that. She wanted to make things right for him, and for the life of him he couldn't figure out why. What made him so special? He was nothing more than a rancher trying to keep afloat.

Her eyes had held a suspicious sheen last night, and he'd thought for a moment or two that she was going to cry. But not Alex. He saw now she was strong, practical. The kind of woman who would face whatever needed facing without histrionics and tissues. The more he knew her, the more he respected her. And the more he found himself daydreaming about her prairie sky-blue eyes and the dark waterfall of her hair.

He swung out of bed, hurriedly pulling on a pair of faded jeans. There was something he needed to take care of—something that had kept him awake in the pale, sun-washed hours of dawn.

He heard her footsteps echo softly to the bathroom down the hall, and he slipped into her room to wait.

When she came back, his heart stopped at the sight she made. She halted her footsteps in surprise, seeing him sitting on the rumpled coverlet of the bed. In no more than a second he saw her tousled hair falling over her shoulders, the pristine white pajama set, which accented the fullness of her breasts and the growing bump at her midsection, and which ended mid-thigh, revealing shapely legs and pretty, dainty feet. The sight of her, fresh from her still-warm bed, made his heart stop.

"G…Good morning," she stuttered in surprise.

At her appearance, he rose, wiping his palms against the thighs of his jeans nervously. "I heard you get up. I hope that's OK?"

"Why wouldn't it be?"

"You're the one standing in the doorway like you're afraid to come in any further."

She *was* afraid. Thoughts of Connor had dominated her dreams, and he had been the first thing she'd thought of upon waking. For him to be here, now, in the quiet morning hours, seemed so…intimate.

She abruptly realized that she was standing in white maternity pajamas which fell a bit shy of modest. Heat flooded her cheeks and down her neck.

He was waiting, and she went the rest of the way in. He took a few steps so that they were scant inches apart.

"What are you doing here?" she whispered, keeping her voice low.

He stepped even closer, so close she had to tilt her neck to look into his face, feeling the heat of his body radiating through the thin cotton she wore.

"Today is the big day," he whispered huskily.

Her head dropped so he couldn't see how flustered she became at the thought. "Everything is ready."

His hand found hers, and he squeezed her fingers. "Except for one thing."

Her eyes darted to his in confusion. This was feeling distinctly like romance, and after having him haunt her dreams she had little defence against him. As she gazed into his face his eyes darkened with something she didn't understand. But when he held her hand that way, and looked deeply into her eyes, her brain simply turned off and she started to babble.

"I can't see how anything is missing. We've seen to the cake, the flowers, the minister—"

"Alex."

She stopped talking and only stared, letting intimacy surround them in the silence. A jolt flashed through her entire body every time he said her name in *that way,* and in admitting it called herself ten times the fool. This wasn't part of the plan at all. She was far more comfortable dealing with Connor when he was being practical and realistic. The memory of saying their promises to each other last night echoed through her brain. It had been a turning point, she realized. For both of them. They'd spoken from their hearts—and she couldn't speak for Connor, but voicing her intentions had made one thing crystal clear to Alex. She loved him. But this was a marriage of convenience only, and her girlish fancies were only serving as a terrible distraction. She had to remember why they were doing this. She had to remember that they needed to stay only friends if she were to come out of this with her heart intact.

"I'm a bit nervous, that's all." Her eyes fell on the closet, where even now her wedding dress hung, white perfection. She felt unworthy of it. Unworthy of him. It was meant to be a symbol of purity, but there was nothing pure about Alexis Grayson. Impoverished, uneducated, pregnant Alex.

In a few short hours she'd be wearing it, carrying a bouquet of roses and gardenia. It seemed like a wild, crazy dream.

"Me too."

His admission, instead of relaxing her, made her fingers curl with tension. Good God, one of them being jittery was bad enough. She'd been counting on him to keep a level head through all of this. She reminded herself yet again why she was doing it. Security was something she'd always craved, and now she knew she was going to be responsible for another life. She owed it to her child. This was all he'd asked of her. It wasn't much; it was too much.

Her hand drifted to her stomach and rested against the small mound there. His eyes softened as he placed his own hand, strong and warm, on top of hers.

"He's growing."

She swallowed and somehow managed to get out, "Every day."

She closed her eyes at the warmth of his hand seeping through her pajamas and into her core. In the time she'd been here he'd never touched her in such a way, or expressed an intimate interest in the life growing within her. The bubble of her belly was firm and taut, and when she opened her eyes his were shining down at her. He understood, she realized. In that moment, with his hand warm on the life she carried, for the first time she wished in her heart that this baby was his. He would be a wonderful father.

He cleared his throat as he removed his hand. "Are you wondering why I'm here?"

Without his touch her skin cooled, leaving her empty. She couldn't get used to that feeling, then. She'd miss it far too much when it was gone.

"Is there something we forgot?"

The hand that had touched her stomach slid up and cupped her neck gently, drawing her forward as her heart thundered. What was he doing? In all their days here together the closest they'd been was that night in his office, and that had been comfort. This didn't feel like comfort. It felt like…passion. Her body trembled beneath his hand. She wasn't prepared for passion. She wasn't prepared for what that might mean. This had to be about maintaining a friendly relationship so no one got hurt at the end. Why was he pulling her close, his gaze fixed on her lips?

"In a few short hours," he murmured, "we'll share our first kiss as husband and wife." His other hand lifted to slide under the hair at her neck. "I don't want our very first kiss to be in front of our guests. Private is much better, don't you think?"

"You… I… Oh, dear."

"I'd like to get it out of the way now," he said, and bent his head.

Her breath slid out, shaky and scared. "Connor," she started to protest weakly, "I don't…" If he kissed her now, she'd be lost completely.

He erased whatever should have come out next by placing his lips gently on hers.

His lips were warm and soft, and she let go of all her fears and misgivings and kissed him back. Greedily she tasted him, her heart leaping as his lips opened and invited her in. Still he was soft, patient, and devastating, as his mouth slid from hers and dropped fleeting kisses on her cheeks, her eyes, the tip of her ear. Oh, goodness, this was no "you may kiss the bride" kiss. This was a "give me five minutes and I'll have you in bed" kiss, and her knees turned to jelly at the thought of the still-warm bed only a few feet behind them. He caught her weight in his arms. Only when she heard herself moan did his mouth return to hers, consuming, leaving her full, then emptying her completely. Heaven. Heaven had to be being kissed by Connor Madsen.

Her arms lifted and wound around his neck, and she pressed herself closer to him, feeling the buffer of the baby between them. She'd never been the kind of woman to dwell on what could never be, not until the baby and Connor. Being with him, close to the life she'd always wanted and never had…something had changed inside her, stopped her from running from feelings and memories and made her sentimental and wistful. At this moment, with his lips warm and loving on hers, she felt the shadow of the girl she'd been in the woman she'd become, and knew the bittersweet pain of wanting what could never be. They had said they would be friends, and it had worked well until today. But from this day forward they would be married, in name only. And with shattering tenderness she tried to wordlessly show him that she would give him everything, if he'd only take it.

Breathing heavily, he pulled away, putting his hands firmly on Alex's shoulders. "God, I'm sorry. I didn't intend for that to happen."

Alex stepped away from his touch, the hands that were still burning fire through her skin. Her body was strangely weightless, humming like a plucked string.

"Me either."

Silence fell, heavy with implications. Because neither of them was saying it had been a mistake. Or expressing regret. Or promising it would never happen again.

"I should go help with chores, since I'm already up."

He made it to the door before he turned back. "Alex?"

"Yes?"

She kept her back to him. She didn't dare face him right now, not with what she knew was nothing other than naked longing on her face, and she incapable of hiding it.

"You're going to make a beautiful bride."

He escaped downstairs while she pressed her fingers to her tingling lips.

By two o'clock, Johanna shooed Alex out of the way. "Everything is ready, and Millie's on her way over with the food. Go start getting ready. I've a surprise coming for you in half an hour."

Alex halted halfway to the stairs. "A surprise? But you've done too much already."

"Hush. Go run yourself a bubble bath."

"Yes, boss," Alex grumbled. Everything was ready…but Alex had never met most of the guests coming today. She wanted everything to be perfect.

If a month ago anyone had told her she'd be soaking in a tub of scented bubbles, preparing for her wedding, she would have had a good laugh. Now she wasn't laughing. Her body was a bundle of nerves. Suddenly this whole marriage thing had changed…since that kiss this morning.

She was sure it had meant more to her than to him. After all, it was easy to get swept away by desire, and she couldn't blame him for that. But as far as deeper feelings…Connor was marrying her to save Windover. She must not forget that. She could feel all she wanted, but she couldn't let herself act on it again. If she did she risked her heart truly being involved, and her heart was already damaged. She'd lost enough. If she could care less, she wouldn't lose as big. Right now she had to think damage control.

Stepping out of the bubbles, she wrapped a thick blue towel around herself and stared in the mirror. Today she was a bride. After tonight she would be Alex Madsen, Connor's wife. Johanna would go home, no longer chaperoning and running interference. And she and Connor would still be sleeping in separate bedrooms.

She dried her hair, letting the natural curl spring free in the silky locks. Her make-up she'd do last, at her dressing table. She slipped from the bathroom into her room.

There was no maid of honor to help her get ready today. Instead she was alone, and strangely she preferred it that way. Away from probing eyes and questions, away from the expected teasing and innuendoes so typical of weddings.

Johanna was downstairs, talking to her friend Millie, the rattle of dishes and happy chatter syncopating the air. Steps came up the stairs, heavy ones. She waited, wrapped only in her towel. Drawers opened and closed with muffled thuds in Connor's room. Yes, things had changed. Even knowing he was on the other side of the wall, and that she was standing nearly naked in a towel, had her pulse leaping erratically in her throat. Girlish fantasies, she chided herself. *Get a grip, girl.* She frowned into the mirror.

Maybe it was just wedding fever. Weddings did strange things to people.

The shower started and she tried *not* to imagine him standing beneath the hot spray.

Dropping the towel, she dressed in the undergarments she'd bought for today. They weren't expensive, or even very fancy, but ordinary white cotton panties, with a swatch of lace at each hip, and a strapless bra, necessary for her growing breasts. She smiled at her reflection. She'd always wanted bigger breasts—but getting pregnant wasn't exactly how she'd planned on getting them.

Soberly she pulled on pantyhose—the control-top type for

this one day, to minimize the bulge at her waist. She took the satin and organza creation from the white bag and stepped into it.

She was struggling with the last three inches of zipper when a knock sounded at the door. "Who is it?" she called. If it were Connor, there was no way she was opening it. The last thing they needed today was bad luck.

"It's Johanna. With your surprise."

Alex opened the door a crack. "OK. You can come in. I need help with my zipper anyway."

Johanna laughed coming in, another younger, absolutely gorgeous woman with her. "Alex, this is Carmen. She's here to fix your hair and makeup."

Alex beamed, holding out a hand. "Nice to meet you. Especially nice since I'm not very good at either hair or makeup."

Carmen smiled. "Your hair is much like mine. Where's your headpiece?"

Johanna connected the hook and eye clasp at the back of the dress. "It's over there, on the bed." She turned Alex to face her. "That dress is perfect. I'll be back after I've dressed. With one more thing."

When Johanna returned, Alex was getting her lips painted. With one last brush, Carmen stood back. "There. You are perfect."

Alex rose, looked in the mirror, and wanted to cry.

Her eyes were large, and somehow more luminous than she could have imagined, while her skin appeared dewy and flawless. Her lips were etched and painted with a colour very close to her natural pigment, and her hair was pulled back gently from the sides, the remainder curling simply down her back. A small circlet of flowers sat daintily on her head, a thin, filmy veil drifting to her waist.

"I look like a bride." She touched a finger to her cheek that glistened with something like glitter. Oh, she'd tried desperately to avoid feeling like a fairytale princess, to stay grounded and realistic. Now her stomach danced with the thought of walking to Connor's side looking this way. What would he think? A flush crept up her neck. After the demonstration she'd put on this morning, he would certainly think she meant this to be a real wedding.

"A very beautiful one," Johanna whispered, and Alex spun to see tears in Johanna's eyes. "Connor won't know what to do with himself."

Alex laughed. After this morning, she knew that Connor would know exactly what to do with himself. But she was pleased, more than pleased, with her appearance. "Thank you so much," she said to Carmen, squeezing her hands. "I love it."

"You are welcome." The woman packed up her bag and smiled on her way out the door. "I'll see you next week, Mrs. Madsen."

"Now. Sit for a moment. I have something for you."

"Something else?" Alex perched on the edge of the stool, facing away from the mirror. "Surely not."

"You know the saying. Something old, something new…"

"Something borrowed, something blue."

"That's right." Johanna pulled over a matching stool and sat, careful not to wrinkle her pale blue suit. She opened her clutch purse and took out a small box. "This should cover the 'borrowed' and 'blue' part."

Alex took the box with shaking fingers. Opening the lid, she found a square velvet box. Inside were nestled a sapphire and diamond necklace and earring set.

"They're gorgeous."

"Lars gave them to me on our tenth anniversary. Connor's mother wore them on her wedding day. And now it is your turn."

Alex carefully removed the earrings, took out her own pearl studs which she had planned on wearing, and replaced them with the antique sapphires. "Oh, Johanna." The oval stones were surrounded by tiny winking diamonds. She held up the necklace and Johanna fastened it around her neck.

"This isn't right. You're making this feel like a real wedding. And these are family heirlooms. It isn't right." She raised her hands, preparing to remove the earrings.

Johanna stopped her with a hand. "You need to keep an open mind."

It's not my mind I'm worried about, it's my heart, she thought wistfully, rising and impulsively hugging the woman she had to struggle to keep from calling Gram.

"Well," she choked, getting a little misty, "I have borrowed, blue, and new. I guess three out of four isn't bad."

"You'll have your fourth, don't worry." Johanna paused by the door. "I'll be back; it's almost time. Once Connor is in place I'll come get you."

She returned quickly. "It's time, Alex. Are you ready?"

Alex nodded. "As ready as I'm going to be."

Johanna smiled. "I've brought your bouquet. And I've got the ring. Connor's already asked me twice."

Neither she nor Connor had any attendants; instead Johanna was serving as their witness, carrying the ring and signing the marriage certificate. Alex followed her down the stairs, out the front door, and around the corner of the house. Connor stood with his back to the guests, chatting with the minister. Alex stared at his back. There was no turning back now. For better or worse they were going through with this sham, and her heart was a tangled mess of guilt and the illusion of romance. She would walk down the grassy aisle between the chairs and meet him, agreeing to spend her life with him. Only she, Connor and Johanna knew it was to be an abbreviated union.

Johanna gave a signal, squeezed Alex's hand, and left to take her seat. As soon as she was seated, Alex heard a guitar start a rendition of Pachelbel's "Canon", and somehow, she wasn't sure how, she made her feet move to the music.

Connor turned when the music started, and she paused as their eyes met. His brows lifted briefly in surprise, then a huge smile of approval swept over his face, the heat of it tangible even from several feet away. Faces turned in her direction, but she focused on none other than Connor and his melted-chocolate eyes as her slippers silently crushed the grass beneath her feet.

She stopped when he took three steps out of position and lifted his hand, offering it to her.

She took it.

"You look beautiful," he whispered, making her heart swell. He led her under the arch and before the minister, to begin their life together.

CHAPTER TEN

THE minister's voice intoned clearly. Numb, Alex's fingers shook in Connor's, her lips quivering as tears trembled on her lashes. To anyone looking on, she looked like a proper, emotional bride, gazing lovingly at her husband-to-be. She *felt* that way, though she didn't have a right to. Didn't have the right to pretend this was real. She was vaguely aware of the small sea of faces looking up at them, at the whisper of the breeze through the thin poplar leaves, of the sound of magpies chattering in the line of trees along the north pasture. She was more aware that Connor was holding her gaze steadily, of the way his suit jacket fit over his broad shoulders, of how he'd missed the tiniest spot shaving just beneath his left ear.

The next ten minutes passed in a haze, a series of impressions that left Alex feeling more and less than she'd expected. The feel of Connor's hand holding hers; the sound of the minister's voice offering a prayer; handing her bouquet off to take his fingers in hers.

She'd expected more clarity, more guilt, more shame. Less emotion, less longing, less love. Then why, oh why, did everything seem so *real*? So right—preordained, even? Was it only because she wanted it to be something it was not?

Then it was done. Connor took a gold band, studded with

a half-dozen tiny diamonds, and slipped it on to her finger, sealing their covenant of lies.

"You may kiss the bride."

That line came through her consciousness crystal clear, and she lifted startled eyes to Connor's. They were warm with understanding and the little secret of the kiss they'd already shared in the weak morning sunlight. *Sealed with a kiss…*

His mouth touched hers, paused, deepened, lingered, until he pulled away just enough that her lips followed ever so briefly. She stared at the fullness of his mouth, smudged with the colour of her lipstick, and her cheeks flamed as clapping erupted.

It was done. In the space of a few minutes and a single kiss she was Mrs. Connor Madsen. She let him take her hand and guide her down the aisle between the seats toward the shaded side of the house.

"Are you OK?"

Connor's voice held more than a trace of concern, and Alex pasted on a smile, holding it there until she was sure it would stay on its own.

"Of course I am."

"You've hardly eaten anything."

There was a very good reason for that. Alex stared down at the sliced beef and potato salad on her plate. Now there was no turning back, and because of it, the gravity of what they were doing had sunk in. The marriage certificate was signed. And even if it hadn't been, she knew she'd made the horrible mistake of giving her heart to a man who didn't want it.

To stop his worrying, she popped a piece of meat into her mouth and chewed. "There. I promise I'm not going to starve."

"You're supposed to be happy."

Connor leaned closer to her bare shoulder as they sat at one of the white-covered tables. To anyone watching it looked like nothing more than a new husband whispering something intimate to his bride, but to Alex it was a knife to the heart. Her wedding day. It *was* supposed to be happy, joyous, carefree. Instead it was bittersweet. Filled with wishes instead of dreams come true.

"I am happy," she lied, still keeping the forced smile in place. "It's been…a little tiring."

His hand rested warmly on her shoulder. Didn't he realize what he was doing to her with every tender glance, every simple touch?

"It won't be much longer." Connor nodded toward the band warming up on the deck, above the makeshift dance floor. "We can have a few dances and disappear."

Her fork clattered to her plate. Disappear? Like brides and grooms did?

"Sure," she choked out, trying desperately to swallow as she started coughing. She reached for her water glass, staring at the gold band winking on her finger. It didn't look like the typical thing Connor would buy. If he'd asked her, she would have said a plain, cheap gold band would have sufficed. She hadn't bought him one at all, and thought now perhaps she should have. But he'd commented once that he didn't wear rings because they were too much of a danger around the farm equipment. She hadn't persisted because in her own mind it would have tied him to her in a way that wasn't real.

The band played a few riffs, the drummer ran a little solo down his set, and the singer stepped up to the mic. "Ladies and gentlemen," he said, gesturing with a hand, "Mr. and Mrs. Connor Madsen!"

Amid the clapping Connor rose and held out his hand. She took it, let him lead her across the lawn to the plywood floor. There he took her into his arms as their guests smiled on.

Alex knew none of them. She'd been introduced after the ceremony, but she was still a stranger in this community where everyone knew everyone else and had for years. It drove home the fact that she didn't belong.

"You look beautiful," Connor murmured in her ear. "In case I haven't told you already."

Oh, his words. They had the power to hurt her now, when she knew he didn't actually mean them. Or perhaps he did mean them, just not the way she wanted him to.

Their feet shuffled to the slow beat of "Amazed", while Connor pulled her closer so that her belly was pressed firmly against him. His suit coat was gone, and the heat of his skin radiated through his white shirt, warming her in the evening cool. He'd loosened his tie, and the warm smell of his aftershave mingled with the scent of the wild roses that grew along the edge of the driveway. Her eyes closed as his fingers tightened around hers, and she rested her head against his shoulder.

I love you, Connor. She spoke the words in her heart, wishing she could say them aloud. How could she not? He was the first person to care about what happened to her in a long time. He was her rock, and she knew deep down she shouldn't rely on him too heavily, seeing as she'd be leaving in a few months. Yet she couldn't help herself. She was tired of being alone. The sigh slipped out before she thought to stop it.

Connor felt the soft breath of her sigh against his neck and swallowed. He wasn't sure how she'd managed it, but what had started out as a fine, sensible, platonic solution wasn't sensible or platonic any longer. He let his fingers slip up her back and under the lush dark curls cascading over her shoulders. Beautiful, and brave—so very brave. She didn't realize it, he bet, but she had that pregnancy glow that grandmothers talked about. A luminescence, a tranquility about her. Had he really thought he could marry her and then let her go? A strictly business arrangement?

Why couldn't there be a way to have both? If the time came and she still wanted out, honor said he'd have to let her go.

But what if he could convince her to stay in the meantime?

The song ended and they pulled apart. Going with instinct, Connor refused to relinquish her hand as she started to step away, instead giving it a tug and pulling her back to his arms. She looked stunned and he smiled, his teeth flashing in the twilight. His eyelids drifted closed and he kissed her.

There'd only been that one kiss under the arch during the ceremony, and he was determined to make this one good. There was clapping and cheering, but Connor blocked it out, urging her to respond, his blood firing recklessly as she finally did, lifting her hand and threading it through his hair as he held her close.

Their mouths parted; Connor gave a last seductive nibble on her lower lip. Her cheeks flamed as red as prairie fire.

"Whoo-eee!" The lead singer made a point of whooping it up. "We'd better have another dance, dontcha think?"

They started another country ballad and other couples joined them on the floor as Connor laughed, his heart lightening a bit. She wasn't immune. That kiss hadn't been faked. Their bodies slid together again, more relaxed.

"Do you like your ring?" he asked in her ear.

Alex looked up at him. "It's beautiful. But I didn't think you were going to buy something this fancy. You didn't need to spend the money…"

On something that was temporary. He heard the end of the sentence as clearly as if she'd spoken it aloud, but he chose to ignore it. "All it cost was a small cleaning bill," he explained, looking down into her eyes. Tiny rhinestones winked within her hair, he marvelled. "This ring belonged to my great-grandmother."

She paled, visibly. "You gave me a family heirloom? Are you crazy?"

He saw her eyes dart to Johanna, who was laughing and chatting with Millie and Reverend and Mrs. Wallace.

"I did. My mother wore it, and as my wife you should too."

"But…but…" She swallowed, then looked him square in the eye. "We both know I'm not really your wife."

"We could ask the minister. I'm pretty sure the certificate is legal."

She laughed in spite of herself. "I'm not sure that's a good idea."

"Don't worry so much."

"Well, if that isn't pot calling kettle," she retorted, leaning back to accuse him with her eyes. "It just doesn't seem right, you know?"

"I wanted you to have it. Right now let's enjoy dancing, OK? I haven't danced with you before, and this should be a night of firsts."

He let his body do the talking then, holding her close and swaying her gently to the music. He looked up; couples glided by them, smiling foolishly at the newlyweds.

The song ended, more beers were popped open at the coolers, and the band started a toe-tapping two-step.

"Come on," he called, tugging her arm, but she resisted.

"I can't."

"What do you mean, you can't?" Everyone and their dog knew how to two-step by the time they hit grade school, didn't they? He tugged her hand again.

"Seriously." Her smile dropped. "I don't know how. And I don't want to embarrass myself." Couples circled the dance floor, turning and stepping, and her eyes widened. "I'll trip everyone up."

He relented, pulling her to the soft grass to the side. "Then you'll have to learn," he answered. "Like this."

He held her in his arms. "You step backward. One, one-two-three, one, one-two-three, so that you keep going in a circle."

She tried it, did it twice, fumbled on the third. "I feel like an idiot."

"You look like an angel," he fired back, putting his hand back on her waist. "One, one-two-three." This time she managed several steps.

"OK. Now in time."

"You mean that wasn't?"

He laughed, full-throated, eyes twinkling. "Honey, that was half-time. We gotta double it up."

And they were off. "Don't look at your feet," he advised. "Relax." They circled around on the grass, her smile growing with each successful step.

"OK. Now we're going to try a turn."

"You're crazy."

"Oops, here we go," he answered, leading her smoothly through the turn. She returned to face him, back in step.

"I did it!"

In her excitement she forgot to one-two-three, her feet stuttering, halting them again. "Darn it."

"It's OK. Here we go again. And this time we'll turn you the other way."

He waited until she was going smoothly, then danced her over to the floor and lifted her up. He nodded to the band to keep going, they joined the circle and two-stepped with the rest.

When it was over, she was breathless and laughing. "That was fun! And I didn't even mess up too much!"

"You hungry now? You didn't eat much at dinner." He placed his hand at her back, feeling the warmth of her skin through the smooth fabric.

"I'm OK. Maybe some water."

They left the group waltzing away and headed to the refreshment table. The first stars were coming out and the air was cooling. Citronella torches lit the perimeter of the celebration area, keeping the mosquitoes at bay and casting a warm flickering glow over the gathering.

"I'm sorry about earlier," she apologized, her hands turning her plastic tumbler around and around.

"I think I understand. It wasn't exactly what it appeared to be, was it?"

"No."

He frowned, unsure of how to proceed. It was too soon. If he did anything silly or sentimental she'd chalk it up to the mood of the day. And she'd be partially right, he admitted to himself. Weddings did bring out the romance in people. But what he had planned was more long-term…a wooing, he supposed, to use an old-fashioned term, and one he'd derided his grandmother for using only weeks ago.

He only had a few months to accomplish it, and he knew he had to make the most of every opportunity, wedding day or not.

"How's Junior holding up? Are you tired?"

"A little. But everyone's still here…"

"We can make our excuses. It's almost—well, expected."

Again the awkward silence.

"Alex, dear." Johanna slid up behind her and squeezed her shoulder. "I must be going. Millie's offered to drive me since…well…" She held up her glass and ice cubes tinkled. "I'm staying there tonight. Wouldn't be right, me staying here."

Alex averted her eyes, embarrassed. It wasn't like this was going to be a typical wedding night of champagne and passion, now, was it? Her body heated with the very thought of it.

Johanna continued on, unfazed. "You made a picture," she beamed. "And you too, Connor."

"You know, Grandmother, it used to be 'Connor dear' and then 'Alex'." He grinned widely. "But then, look at her," he went on, dropping his eyes to his wife's profile. "Today, she *should* come first."

Alex snorted, making light of his gallantry, yet unable to hide the telltale blush that bloomed on her cheeks.

"Get used to it, dear boy." Johanna winked at Alex outrageously. "But you should probably throw the bouquet soon, don't you think?"

Alex nodded, not sure whether to be relieved the day was drawing to a close or to resent the fact that she was being told what to do *again*. For the most part she hadn't minded someone else taking the lead, relieving her of some of the responsibilities and decisions, but she'd been on her own long enough that at times it chafed.

Johanna left to notify the band, and Connor retrieved her bouquet from the table. "This is your last official duty of today," he commented. "Then we can disappear if you want."

The band leader called for all the single ladies, then held out his hand to help Alex up the stairs to the deck. She let the roses fly, straight into the hands of a pretty young blond with roses in her cheeks.

Duties done, Connor danced one more dance with his wife, then shepherded her to the front door, lifted her in his arms, and carried her over the threshold.

CHAPTER ELEVEN

"PUT me down, you idiot!"

Alex's laughter echoed through the dim foyer as she squirmed in his arms. Goodness, he'd lifted her as though she were as light as a feather, the warmth of his body flooding through her as her arms looped around his neck instinctively. Her heart raced at being in his arms, even if he were only acting silly.

They smiled at each other a long time, until Connor quietly commented, "It's good to hear you laugh."

"I haven't done it much lately. Neither have you."

"Perhaps now we can change that," he remarked, taking a step toward her.

Her heart leapt in her chest as he approached, but he merely passed by her and went to the fridge.

"The music will go on for another hour. Why don't you go change out of your dress? There's something I wanted to do earlier that I forgot."

She was about to refuse when the band began another song, the bass and drums pounding loudly, quelling any argument she might have made for retiring. "Oh, all right," she relented, heading for the stairs.

She struggled with the zipper at the back of her dress for nearly five minutes, but she'd be darned if she'd ask for his help. After that kiss on the dance floor, and the way he'd looked at her all night, the last thing she needed was his help undressing.

She paused, her hands splayed across her burgeoning belly, assessing. Before too long it would be very clear why they'd got married, and everyone would think the baby was Connor's. What, then, would people think when a few months after he or she was born they separated and she left with the child?

And why in the world was she worried about what others would think? It had never mattered before—but then she'd never let herself rely on anyone before either. She'd only had herself to worry about. She was finding that not being alone, even temporarily, was a big adjustment.

Alex pulled on baggy sweatpants and a sweatshirt. She hung up the dress carefully, running her fingers over the bodice wistfully. Oh, what a wedding day. And what a laughable wedding night. Alex in shabby clothes while her new husband made a midnight snack. Not a candle or bottle of champagne in sight. No white silk lingerie or rose petals spread on the bed.

When she returned downstairs the band was still playing and laughter echoed throughout the yard. Connor was placing wine goblets on the table. She followed and sat down.

"You look comfortable."

"I suppose." She helped herself to a strawberry from a small dish he'd placed in the middle of the table and dipped it in yogurt. "What do you think they'd say—" she gestured toward the backyard with her strawberry "—if they could see us now?"

His tie was gone and his shirt unbuttoned. Casually he twisted the top off a bottle of sparkling grape juice.

"Who cares? I didn't do this for them."

"Then who did you do it for?"

Brown eyes clashed with hers in the gray light. The longer he was silent the more she was drawn in, until she almost

believed he'd done it for her. But that was silly. She'd told him
already that a simple Justice of the Peace would have sufficed.

"For Windover," he said finally, settling back in his chair.

Of course. And she'd done it for the security of her child.

She picked another berry off the platter. "Thank you for everything you've done," she said, more strongly than she felt.
She had to be realistic. That kiss during the dance had been
merely for show, to avoid unpleasant questions. She understood that now. Nothing in the situation had changed, besides
the fact that she had feelings that she couldn't reveal without
making everything go pear-shaped. "Let's hope things go
smoothly from here on in."

He poured the liquid into the glasses. "I knew you couldn't
have champagne, but I wanted us to have a toast. It only
seemed right." He recapped the bottle and chuckled. "A twist
off top, though. Reminds me of college days."

He was trying to keep things light; the least she could do
was go along. "A lovely vintage, I'm sure."

He handed her the glass, standing close by her side. "To
the beginning of a great future, for both of us."

She raised her glass with a shaky hand, touching the rim to
his before drinking. She should offer something in response,
but everything she wanted to say would come out wrong.

She remembered looking up at the sky and seeing the first
star appear earlier.

"To dreams coming true."

She closed her eyes and made a brief wish in her heart.

She'd put such childish things behind her long ago, but
now, with so much at stake, she dared fate.

"To dreams," he answered, touching her glass in response.

Alex woke late, past nine, to dim light and the sound of rain
spattering against her window. Connor would have been up
ages ago, despite the late hour they'd gone to bed, and she'd

fully meant to get up at the usual time and make breakfast. He wouldn't be haying today, she realized.

Now that the wedding was over, she got out the clothes she'd been hiding—maternity jeans and a cute stretchy T-shirt in pale yellow that would grow with her over the coming months. She examined herself in the mirror. More comfortable, yes, but also very clear now that she was expecting. It was a relief and a strain all at once. But she couldn't hide it forever.

At the bottom of the stairs she was surprised to see Connor sitting at the table, drinking coffee.

He looked up as she stepped inside and smiled, a slice of warmth that made her tingly all over as his eyes assessed her new clothing.

"Well, well. I bet that feels better."

"Much."

"No more popping buttons or strained zippers?" He lifted his coffee cup, eyes twinkling above the rim.

"No, but thanks for pointing that out."

She went to the fridge, took out the milk and poured a glass for herself.

"A lot of men find pregnant women extremely attractive."

And would you be one of them? The question popped into her mind but not out of her mouth. Innuendoes had no place now. The most important thing was to keep things friendly and remember the end goal. Security for her baby, prosperity for Windover, and her heart left intact.

"It's probably something about the so-called 'glow'."

"I suppose. But it's more than that." He abandoned playing with his mug for a moment and studied her earnestly. "There's something about a woman, knowing she's carrying life inside her, nurturing it, loving it… It's…" His voice dropped off.

Despite the discomfort she was feeling at the moment, she urged him to continue. "It's what?"

"Sacred."

He rose and put his cup in the dishwasher, avoiding her gaze, and she knew he'd revealed more than he intended. Goodness, he couldn't be fighting attraction too, could he?

Of course not. That was more wishful thinking on her part.

When he turned back his cheeks were more relaxed, eyes friendly. "I didn't mean to be backward in paying a compliment," he explained. "What I meant to say is…I hope you're not self-conscious about it. You look wonderful."

She had been getting over the self-conscious bit—until now, that was, and she turned away before he saw her embarrassment.

"Have you been out to the barns already?" She changed the subject.

"Mike did the chores again, as a wedding present, so I slept in."

Despite her fatigue, sleep had been long in coming, and she wondered if it had for him as well. Had he lain on his side of the wall with wishes of his own? Had he been thinking, as she had, about what she'd always hoped her wedding would be? The real one, not the acting job they'd done yesterday. Although at times it hadn't felt much like acting…

"I've got meetings in Leduc this afternoon. I'm going to shower—unless you want to go first?"

"No, I'll clean up, I think," she replied, waving her hand at the leftover mess from the previous day. Empty trays littered the back counter, and their fruit platter and wine glasses sat partially full from their midnight repast. "Your grandmother will be coming back for her things, too."

It was a reminder that after this morning they'd be living here alone, unchaperoned. It added a degree of intimacy, an *element*, that lived and breathed as tangibly as both of them.

"By the way, the rodeo is next week." He shoved his hands in his pockets. "Don't make any plans, OK? I want to take you to the finals at least. It's a fun time."

She'd never been to a rodeo in her life. Her only experience with it had been changing the channel when the Calgary Stampede coverage came on in the summer. Men in dirty boots and cowboy hats, getting on livestock that *smelled* and getting knocked off. She smiled weakly. "I'm not sure rodeo's my thing."

His smile faded so quickly she knew she'd end up going just out of guilt.

"At least think about it." His voice had cooled considerably. "Everyone from around here goes. It might look funny if you didn't."

She fought the urge to remind him it had only been the previous night that he had said he didn't care what people thought. She certainly didn't want to start an argument only one day after their wedding.

He jogged up the stairs two at a time while she blew out a breath, wondering how they were going to stumble their way through the next six months if already they were tiptoeing around each other, dissecting words.

He shut his binder and pushed back his chair now that the meeting was over. His thoughts should have been about the dire news he'd received today…but all he could think about was how he'd bungled things with Alex this morning.

First of all he'd gone on and on about how beautiful pregnant women were, then he'd got shot down about the rodeo. He'd forgotten, quite simply, that she wasn't a rancher's wife. She'd have no interest in rodeo, and the original agreement was only short term, so why would she bother putting herself out? She didn't want to stay here, so why did he want to convince her to stay?

He cared about her. He wasn't made to live alone, without being surrounded by family, and being with Alex felt *right*.

If she didn't want to go to the rodeo, he shouldn't press. As he packed up his briefcase, he realized that maybe she was self-conscious about the state of her pregnancy. Of the questions that would arise from relative strangers. It had probably been insensitive of him to mention it. But if he hadn't... He didn't want it to seem like he didn't want to take her anywhere. To keep her hidden.

"Oh, for Pete's sake," he muttered, scowling. Would he walk on eggshells for the next months, worried about making the wrong move? It had never been hard for him to make the difficult decisions before. He'd always been the strong one.

But the stakes were higher this time, and for the first time in his life he admitted something to himself. Something he'd avoided acknowledging throughout his grief for his family, or during the whole ranch crisis. Something he would never have disclosed to another living soul.

He was scared.

The evening was quiet, with only the fading sounds of the birds echoing through the soft twilight. Connor had disappeared after dinner, taking the ATV and going to the south pasture to check on stock. Now that the kitchen was cleaned up, Alex eschewed television, or even a book, and instead sat rocking gently in the porch swing, listening to the sounds of impending night and watching the moon rise off to her left.

Connor had worried about her feeling isolated out here in the middle of nowhere, but the brittle truth was that she'd felt far more alone in the various cities where she'd lived. She knew now that *people* did not cure loneliness. Only one thing did, and that was belonging.

But for how long?

There was an owl somewhere close by, his call echoing plaintively as she caught sight of low headlights approaching from the pasture. Soon after the drone of the ATV engine reached her ears, then muted as it disappeared behind one of the barns. Minutes later Connor appeared as she rocked the swing with a bare toe, sending it swaying gently back and forth.

"Everything OK?"

"Yeah. What a night."

"I know." She smiled up at him, pointing. "There's an owl over there somewhere."

Suddenly a sorrowful howl threaded through the silence. "Do the coyotes bother you?"

The toe kept the swing going. "No. I think they sound wild and beautiful."

She patted the swing beside her, inviting him to sit. He did, the swing creaking beneath the increased weight. Just having him this close warmed the air around her, raising the hairs on her arms. She stroked her fingers down her arm, and without a word Connor rose, grabbed an oversized fleece from the hook inside the door, and handed it to her.

"Thanks."

He sat again, and they rocked in companionable silence as the night deepened and the coyotes howled plaintively.

It was a marvel how they could sit and not feel the need to speak. It was one of the things she most enjoyed about his company. It was comfortable.

"I've thought about the rodeo. I'd like to go, if you still want me to."

His body stayed still, but his head turned to the side, watching her. "You don't have to if you don't want. I don't want to pressure you."

"It would look odd if I didn't."

"So what? That doesn't matter. And there will likely be questions that you may not want to answer. I don't want to put you in that position."

"Are you saying you don't want me to go?" She met his eyes earnestly. "I can understand that. I mean, it's not like I'm going to be here that long. If you want to keep it low-key…"

He flinched. "That's not what I meant at all. I want you to be comfortable. You're welcome to come or not. It's up to you."

Now the silence was awkward and heavy.

After a few minutes he spoke. "This is the damnedest thing."

"I know." The swing creaked softly as it rocked back and forth. Alex kept her gaze fixed on the white moon as it rose across the prairie.

"Married, but not married. Stumbling around trying to make sure we say the right thing. Perhaps it would be better if we were just honest."

Fat chance. Alex knew she couldn't tell him how she felt. Not with their agreement being what it was. If he thought it was awkward now, what would it be like if she unburdened herself only to hear that he didn't feel the same?

"How honest?"

He laughed a little. "How about, I'd like you to come with me on Saturday, but I understand if you don't want to."

He was way too devastating when he laughed like that, his eyes sparkling darkly.

"I'd like to come. It'll be something new."

"About the questions you might face…"

Alex smiled, so widely he goggled. "What's so funny?"

"Nothing," she breathed, touching her hand to her tummy. "Oh, my."

"Alex?"

"The baby's moving." Her grin was a wide hosanna of joy. "Oh, Connor. I thought the last few days it was gas." She laughed. "But this is definitely it."

Instinctively she reached out and grabbed his hand, placing the wide palm on her hard cotton-covered tummy. "There. No, wait." She adjusted his hand, ignoring the startled expression that widened his eyes and flattened his chin.

He stared at his hand, then looked up to meet her gaze.

"Wait. She's really moving now."

"She?" He cocked his head inquisitively. "You think it's a girl? I thought you thought it was a boy?"

"Why would you think that?"

"That night in the den. You said, 'He's growing'."

"Well, I can't exactly call my child 'it' can I? For some reason I think now that she's a she. Mother's prerogative," she added with a smile. Alex couldn't explain it fully, but lately, as her shape had changed, she had a feeling that it was her little girl in there.

His hand was spreading its warmth, and she loved how it felt, solid and sure. If she had her wish, he would be the father to her baby. She removed his fingers, lifted up her T-shirt a few inches, and put his wide hand back on her bare skin.

The baby responded, sending a butterfly vibration skittering against their flattened hands. Connor's gaze flew up to hers.

"That is the most incredible thing I've ever felt," Connor whispered hoarsely. "What does it feel like inside?"

She shifted her shoulder so she was leaning more against him, the pose both intimate and comfortable. "I don't know. Sort of like a gas bubble rolling around, only bigger. Like…" *Like the butterflies I got when you first kissed me,* she thought.

"Like what?" His breath was warm against her hair.

"Like Christmas."

He smiled. She felt it against her scalp even though she couldn't see his face.

His hand shifted, still beneath the hem of her T-shirt, the tips of his fingers slipping cautiously beneath the waistband of her jeans.

It would take no more than a slight turn and she could fit against him. Kissing him. Feeling his hands on her skin, where she so desperately wanted them. Carnal. There was no other word for the way she felt right now. Pregnant or not.

But she'd die before making the first move.

CHAPTER TWELVE

HIS body was so close and warm that it was hard to think, and she scrambled to think of a topic to change the subject. She started to panic, until a single thought popped into her brain and she blurted it out. "So, you told me once that you wanted to be a vet before the accident. Why didn't you? What held you back?"

It was a good question, it turned out. The shift was complete, and he drew back a little. The cool night air pricked up goose-bumps on her skin and she turned to look up into his face.

"And what would I have done with the farm, the herd?" His eyes evaded hers, staring out into the inky blackness as the moon went beneath a cloud. "The whole plan had been for Dad and Jim to run things while I did the schooling, set up the practice here, then Dad would slowly phase out into retirement and Jim and I would run things together. I couldn't just abandon Windover. I love it here. It fell to me to look after it."

"And you always take your responsibilities seriously."

"That's why they're responsibilities."

Alex heard the sad note in his voice and smiled. "I, for one, am glad of it, because you've saved me from being in quite a pickle."

He adjusted his arm, pulling her more securely into the curve of his shoulder. "I like having you here—or hadn't you noticed?"

"You were lonely."

His voice came out over top of her hair, quiet against the wistful howl of coyotes on the hunt again.

"Yes, I was."

She hesitated before asking the next question, wanting to know, afraid of prying too deeply.

"Did…did you get to see them? To say goodbye?"

She felt his throat constrict, bob against her head, and she wondered if she'd indeed gone too far by asking such an intimate question. But all he said was a soft, "Yes."

She reached over and squeezed his hand, the one that moments ago had been resting on the soft stretched skin of her tummy. "Then you're lucky. I didn't. They only found—" She stopped, had to swallow against the painful constriction in her throat. This was silly. She hadn't gotten emotional over it for years. But Connor seemed to have the knack of bringing all her emotions shimmering just beneath the surface. She cleared her throat.

"They only found pieces of the plane and some…some body parts. I never had that chance. I wish I had. I wish I could have been prepared."

"Nothing prepares you for having your life ripped away from you," he murmured huskily.

"Suddenly I just resented so much, you know? Don't get me wrong. I've seen some pretty cool things, being the daughter of historians who traveled. But I guess we always want what we don't have. What I wanted was a regular life. A school year where I had perfect attendance. A mom who baked cookies for my lunch or was my Girl Guide leader. I wanted something more…normal."

"Stable and secure?"

"Yes."

"And then you sacrificed your own dreams just to stay afloat?"

"Sounds familiar, doesn't it, Connor?" She smiled against

the side of his chest and felt rather than heard his soft chuckle as he silently conceded her point.

"So, Alex Grayson Madsen, what did you *want* to do?"

She perched up on her elbow and aimed an impish grin at him. "You ready?" At his nod, she continued. "I wanted to study to be a chef."

He laughed, the feeling warm and welcome. When her giggles joined his, his heart was lighter than it had been in a long time.

Their laughter faded to smiles, the smiles to soft gazes. Soul-baring didn't come easy to either of them, Connor realized. But they'd taken a step tonight. A step to understanding. A step to trusting. He stared at her full, soft lips, wondered how they would taste if he touched his mouth to hers.

"Alex."

He murmured it, sexy-soft, giving her hand a tug until she rested more closely against his chest. She shuddered as he leaned forward, his hair brushing against hers. The combination smelled like flowers and hay. The baby moved against his hand again as his lips nuzzled her earlobe and up along the side, making all the nerve-endings in her neck tighten with anticipation. Instinctively she moved her head against his ear, silently asking for more.

Connor's heart pounded heavily. Never in a million years had he considered that he'd be terrified of touching his own wife, or humbled at feeling a baby kick beneath his hand, especially one not his own.

But he was feeling both awe and need, and he took it slowly, nibbling on her ear, feeling all the electric parts where their bodies touched. She turned her head into his and he brushed light kisses against her jaw. When her weight shifted slightly, he let his hand slide to cradle her ribs intimately.

He sensed her fear and longing, recognizing it because he felt it himself. He couldn't meet her eyes, too afraid that she'd break away if he gave her the chance. With his right arm he pressed gently, until she turned into his body, and then he kissed her like he'd wanted to all day.

Connor was determined to coax her, yet it wasn't necessary as her warm lips met his equally, hungrily. She wanted him, he realized with a start. Without convincing or coercion. His breath came out with a rush and he pulled her up so she lay firmly across his chest, his hand threading through her hair to hold her head in place while his tongue swept into her mouth.

The coyotes howled and his heart sang as she pressed closer to him and his hand slid down over her shoulder, settling just under her arm, with his thumb grazing her full breast. Their cores were pressed together, the firmness of her swollen belly against the taut zipper of his jeans so that she was in no doubt of what was happening to him. Their lips parted and he slid his tongue seductively down the column of her neck.

"I want you," he groaned against her skin, the blood pounding through him furiously. He was sure she could feel a pulse from every inch of his body.

She moaned and arched and he slid up a bit, putting his arms beneath her knees as if to lift her.

"Stop," she breathed raggedly, but his answer was to kiss her again.

She pulled away. "Connor, stop. *Please.*"

He froze, struggling to breathe.

Finally her eyes met his. They were wide, the pupils dark with arousal and tinged with fear.

"I can't…"

"Can't?" He said it softly, but it came out strained. So much at stake, fraught with complications, but all he was thinking about right now was taking her upstairs and loving her thoroughly. He shouldn't feel this attraction, not after this brief amount of time, and not when she was pregnant with another man's baby. Heck, he wasn't even sure if she was still in love with the father or not, and all he could to think about was kissing the wounded look off her face.

She pushed herself out of his arms, staring at him now with something akin to panic. He didn't adjust his position. He stayed half reclined on the swing, hiding nothing from her.

"It's too soo…I mean, it's too much," she stammered, her face white in the moonshine.

"You were going to say it's too soon." He blinked slowly, holding her tethered with his eyes. "Which means you want to."

She backed up a few steps and her eyes skittered away. "It's far more complicated than that."

"You're my wife."

Alex's eyes snapped to his, something in her clicking into place at the warm, proprietary tone in his voice. She wanted to believe. But that was the whole problem. She wanted to believe so much that she wasn't sure she could be objective. She could be only hearing what she wanted to hear. She wanted Connor to want her to stay, but by his own admission he hadn't been in a relationship for a while. It was only natural to get caught up in their situation wasn't it? But what would happen later? What if he changed his mind, realizing that he didn't want to be married to her anymore?

There was too much at stake to let this progress into something that would only be temporary. And leaving after knowing what it was like to make love to him would be unbearable.

She had to take a step back.

"In name."

His eyes cooled, hot magma to cold ash. "Right."

"Look, it's a hard situation…" She blushed at his snort of sarcasm at her terminology. "We got caught up in the moment, that's all."

"Sure. The moment." He pushed himself up, sitting on

the swing now with an unreadable expression masking his face.

"It's simply not sensible, Connor. Surely you can see that? We made an agree—"

"An agreement, yeah-yeah," he broke in impatiently. "I know all about the agreement. I thought It up, remember?"

"You're angry."

He sighed, running his fingers through his hair. It fell raggedly around his face and she wondered how any woman remained immune to him, the way his eyes glowed brown and gold in the moonlight, how he always seemed to have that sexy shadow of stubble by the end of the day…

She shook her head. *Big picture, big picture,* she repeated to herself.

"I'm frustrated. We both know this has gone beyond friendship. Even if you try to deny it, you know it's true."

Her mouth opened and shut like a fish in a bowl. He rose from the swing, and briefly Alex was reminded of a mountain lion, strong, sinuous, stalking its prey. She was helpless as he took slow, deliberate steps until he stood before her, tall, imposing, hard, sexy as sin. Her throat closed over as she tried to swallow. How hard would he press his case? And how strong was she to resist?

His hand, warm and callused, gently cupped the soft skin of her jaw, and her breath came in shallow gasps. She must not, could not, do anything she'd regret.

"Do you know how beautiful you are in the moonlight?" His voice was husky, intimate.

She said nothing, determined to stand her ground, knowing if she spoke she'd say something that would play right into his hands.

"I haven't been able to stop thinking of you since that kiss on our wedding day. But you know that, don't you?"

Dear Lord, he was trying to seduce her, and doing a most

fine job of it. Of course she knew, because she'd done nothing but think of him either. She wanted to believe him. The risk-taker in her begged to be freed, to let go and see where it led.

But she was something else now too—a mother. And the baby inside her demanded that she use caution. To be sure. Right now she was sure of two things. She was sure she was in love with him already, and she was sure he wanted her. But beyond that she wasn't sure he loved her, wasn't sure he wanted her to stay here forever. She didn't trust it because she wanted it too much. And taking a risk on love wasn't something she was equipped to do—not anymore.

She calmly reached up, removed his hand, and stepped back.

"I know you want me. But wanting me isn't enough. I have a child to consider. *My* baby. I won't complicate things further than they are already complicated by sleeping with you."

She reached out and placed a hand on his forearm, not wanting him to go away mad.

"Friends, remember? Helping each other. Caring for each other. That's what I need right now. And that's what you need too."

He looked past her shoulder, out toward the mountains that hulked black in the distance. "You're right, of course," he replied, his voice strangely thick. "Caught in the moment."

He turned away, back into the house, leaving her shivering in the night air and more confused than ever.

Solicitous.

That was the word to describe his behavior toward her over the past week. Polite, kind, solicitous. But never intimate. There was nothing to fault in his treatment of her, nothing at all. Yet something was missing. A spark, that hint of something more, that had kept her looking forward to seeing him and dreading it at the same time. She missed it. But it was what she'd asked for.

She zipped up her jeans, pulling her pink maternity top over the waistband. It wasn't exactly what she imagined people wore to the rodeo, but she didn't exactly have an extensive wardrobe. Connor had said jeans were fine, not everyone dressed in cowboy boots and black hats. He'd smiled when he'd said it, but the old teasing was gone.

Had she hurt his feelings so much? It was difficult to imagine. You could only hurt people you cared about, and she wasn't at all sure of him. More than likely it was his male pride she'd wounded. Yes, that was a much more reasonable explanation for his icy, polite manner of late.

"Alex? You ready?"

Connor's voice echoed up the stairs and she looked in the mirror one last time. Her first public appearance as Connor's wife, and now everyone would know she was pregnant.

Everyone would think it was his.

For the first time she realized that today was going to be difficult for him too. He wouldn't admit to the baby being someone else's, so he was going to have to pretend to be a happy expectant father. Or would he? How was he going to react? She wished now that they'd discussed it, but things had been cool and reserved lately, not exactly the best atmosphere for a heart-to-heart.

No matter. Whatever happened today, it was going to take a great deal of acting ability on both their parts.

Downstairs, he was waiting impatiently in the foyer, looking handsomer than she'd ever seen him. Snug jeans fit down his long legs, a white shirt with blue vertical stripes tucked into the waistband, emphasizing the breadth of his chest and shoulders. He wore boots on his feet and held a black hat in his hand.

He was, she discovered, a cowboy at heart.

"I brought you your sweater. The breeze is chilly today."

"Thank you," she murmured, taking it from his outstretched hand. Her eyes lifted of their own accord and met his. For some silly reason she wanted to say *I'm sorry,* although she couldn't have said why. Instead she slid her arms through the sleeves and grabbed the tiny purse she was taking, sliding out the door before him.

The drive to the rodeo grounds was quiet and blessedly short. As Connor found a place to park, she stared at the wedding ring on her finger and broached the subject that had been on her mind the whole drive.

"People are going to notice. Are you OK with that?"

His eyes were glued to the sideview mirror. "I don't have much choice, unless I keep you hidden from now until Christmas."

Ouch. Honesty hurt.

"What I mean is, are you up to answering the questions they're going to ask?"

"Are you?"

"I don't know. I somehow think it'll be easier for me. I'm the pregnant one. The baby is mine. You married me. There'll be some talk about the rushed marriage, but..." She paused as he turned off the ignition and looked over at her. "But you're going to get congratulated on being the father. It might be hard for you to pretend everything is what it seems."

If she only knew.

The truth was, every question was going to be a reminder that the baby *wasn't* his. A slap in the face. And he'd feel it as acutely as he'd felt her rejection last week. Even if her logic had been dead on, it had still hurt. Because he'd fallen for her. And everywhere he turned these days he found reminders that their time together wasn't permanent.

He'd thought that the chemistry between them would have been enough to bridge the gap, for him to work on her, to make her see that he didn't want her to leave. Instead she'd shot him down and left his head spinning.

"I can handle it."

"Then I can too." She attempted a confident smile that fell flat.

He didn't answer, but got out of the truck, came over to her side and helped her down. "Here we go," he said quietly, taking her hand and leading her toward the entrance.

All eyes were on them as they approached the grandstand. Eyes darted instantly to her midsection, and Alex felt like her lips were permanently stretched and superglued into position. Connor held her hand steadily and nodded hello to neighbors and acquaintances.

He leaned over and whispered in her ear. "Do you want to sit down? You might feel less conspicuous."

"Won't that look silly?"

He tugged her hand, pulling her close. "Not when the events are going to start any minute. Try to relax and have fun."

He found them seats midfield and crossed a booted ankle over his knee. The announcer started up, his deep voice carrying over the loudspeakers with an auctioneer-like twang.

It was fun, all of it. Alex found herself leaning on the edge of her seat during the barrel racing, laughing outrageously at the crash-helmeted children "mutton busting", giggling as one after another the woolly sheep rid their backs of their cargo. She gasped at the bareback broncs and snorted with fun at the wild cow milking competition.

During the saddlebroncs, Connor nudged her arm. "You hungry or thirsty? I thought I might go grab something."

Alex looked around. The stands were jam-packed in the warm June sun, many heads shaded with cowboy hats and hands holding plastic cups of beer or the traditional beef-on-a-bun sandwiches. The scent of the beef did nothing for her and she smiled faintly. "Something cold to drink might be nice."

"Do you want to come with me?"

Her legs were stiff from sitting most of the afternoon, but

then she thought of all the neighbors and townspeople, waiting to ask questions, and decided against. "I think I'll wait here, if it's all the same to you," she answered, trying to smile.

She immediately regretted that choice once he was gone. Alex hadn't quite realized how much she'd relied on the security and protection his presence provided. Now, sitting alone as one by one the riders flew off their horses and into the dusty ring, she felt eyes on her, assessing, calculating. The shape she'd hidden very successfully was now out in the open, and she knew that minds were counting calendars and speculating about the happy event.

Not one person here had heard a whisper of Connor having a relationship, let alone a baby on the way. Now suddenly within a month he was here, married, and with a clearly pregnant wife. She felt every unasked question closing her in until she knew she had to move or scream.

And she'd left Connor to field those questions alone.

She waited several more minutes, feeling like she was in a fishbowl with the water draining fast. As the bull riding began, she left her seat and went to find him.

She caught sight of him from behind at first, standing to one side, a plastic cup in one hand and a bottle of water in the other. His weight was on one hip and she remembered being pressed close to him only a few nights ago, his body hard and sure against hers. He was talking to a young bronc rider who was laughing, his shaggy, copper-colored hair pressed into a sweaty circle from the hat he held in his hand, his jeans sporting one long brown streak of dust.

As she approached from behind the beer tent, she caught the rollicking sound of the man's laugh. "Damn, but that horse was scary. I lasted all of four seconds."

"That's longer than usual, if what the women around here say is true," Connor jabbed, and the man laughed, his teeth even whiter against the dust coating his face.

"Yeah, but what a ride."

She watched Connor take a drink, scuffing his boot in the dirt as he laughed.

Alex stopped. She shouldn't eavesdrop, she knew that. But Connor's voice was rich and low, that same tone that normally sent shivers up her spine.

She retreated behind the beer tent.

She didn't want to hear what answers he provided to the questions that were sure to follow. How many of his neighbors, his associates, had stopped him today and asked about his pregnant wife? He'd been gone over half an hour. How many times had he been expected to show excitement about being a father? How much had he had to pretend that he was in love with his wife? All the while knowing he was lying to their faces?

She couldn't do it anymore.

Her baby deserved more than a mother who lied for money, and that was exactly what it came down to. The longer she stayed, the more lies piled one on top of the other until there was no telling them apart. The beginning and the platonic marriage, then lying to herself that it was all right. Lying to Connor now about her true feelings. Living in constant fear of the truth.

Her stomach lurched painfully; she swallowed back the tears gathering in her throat. It wouldn't do to be caught crying at the rodeo. A bubble of hysterical laughter rose. That sounded exactly like one of the country songs Connor was always playing on the radio. She stepped back, unsure of what to do next.

She couldn't go back to her seat, not alone and not like this. She didn't have keys to the truck, so she couldn't go home. Instead she walked back to the abandoned parking area, toward the pickup under the poplar tree. Her hands shook as she lifted the lever for the tailgate, lowered it down, and hopped up.

Alex slid to the middle of the box, lowered her head to her knees, and tried valiantly not to cry.

She failed.

CHAPTER THIRTEEN

HER seat was empty.

She must have gotten tired of waiting for him. The bull riding was still ongoing, but had to be finishing soon. She couldn't have gone far...

He wandered around for a good ten minutes before he finally thought to check the truck.

His heart leapt to his throat at the sight of her crouched in the back of the truckbed.

"Alex?"

She lifted her head, tendrils of hair straggling around her cheeks.

She'd been crying. A flash of anger shot through him at whoever had said something to make her cry. He shouldn't have left her alone for so long. Lord only knew what questions she'd been asked. He'd fielded his share, and was left feeling a bit raw as a result.

"What's wrong?"

She straightened, pushed back her hair behind her ears, and wiped her cheeks with her fingers. "Nothing."

"You never cry. You hate crying." He remembered her saying that the night of the ruined meal, and said it with a smile, trying to cajole her out of her tears.

He hopped up on the tailgate and started to approach the back of the truckbed, where she was huddled. He halted when he saw what looked like accusation on her face. Was she mad at *him?*

"Honey?"

"I'm not your honey." She lifted her head, sniffed once, effectively shutting him out. "I'd like to go home now, please. I have a headache."

She was downright frosty, and he took off his hat, squatting down a few feet away from her.

"I'm sorry I left you so long. I got talking and…"

"I know."

The words came out bitingly cold and he froze. "You saw me?"

"I did."

She saw the guilt spread over his face, the way he averted his eyes suddenly and his cheeks flushed. She had to be careful, very careful. She hadn't really heard anything, but by his reaction she knew that he'd been asked those horrible, awkward questions.

The very reason she was upset was the reason that she couldn't tell the truth. It wasn't that he'd left her alone. It was carrying guilt around like a noose around her neck. It was that she knew once and for all that her feelings were unrequited, and it made her more vulnerable than ever before. She should have walked away that first moment he'd had those yellow roses in his hands.

She'd allowed herself to get her hopes up. He'd called her his wife, kissed her, held her. Was she wrong in her interpretation of that? Then, on the other hand, he'd said he was sticking to their original agreement. This had all been a horrible mistake—she knew that now—and somehow she had to fix it. Right after she said her piece.

"What did you hear?" His voice was quiet, and a bit wary, and she bravely met his eyes, giving him the only answer she could.

"You told, didn't you? You told our secret. I thought it was only going to be you, me and your grandmother. It wasn't for everyone to know."

Connor looked around, then leaned closer, not wanting this conversation to be heard by the general population.

"I didn't say a word, I swear. I wouldn't do that."

"That's hardly the point now, is it?" She sniffed again, eyes clear of any tears now. She knew that she sounded unreasonable but seemed unable to stop. "I realized something today. It's different for you. Not that it should be, mind you, but once word of this gets out I'll be judged. I'll be completely humiliated! A pathetic loser! So desperate I'd sell my soul to a complete stranger! You'll be poor Connor, taken in by that money-grubber. Because eventually the truth *will* come out, Connor. And I can't live with that lie any longer. I can't pretend for the world that this is some perfect marriage. Someday you'll let it slip. You won't mean to. But you will."

It didn't occur to her that perhaps she was being a tad melodramatic. Instead she was stripped of her pride, laid bare as the impostor she knew she was. The salt in the wound was that she wasn't as cold and heartless as she appeared. Her feelings ran deep; her wants and desires, longings and fears.

Reduced to this.

"I won't tell, I promise. You can trust me."

"Right."

Connor looked around him; the crowd was milling about now that the afternoon events were completed. Unless they wanted a scene in front of half the town, it would be better altogether if they left now.

"Let's finish this at home, OK? In private. I'm assuming you don't want this to be overheard?"

She ignored the hand he offered her, instead getting to her feet and hopping out of the back of the truck without assistance. He followed her, opening her door and shutting it behind her before jogging around to the driver's side and getting in.

She stared out the window as she spoke to him. "This isn't over, you know. I still have a lot more to say."

"I'm sure you do."

He pulled out of the lot, letting the radio do the talking in the tense silence.

Alex stared straight ahead. She couldn't look at him. If she did she knew she'd lose her nerve. She needed to remain cool and objective right now, the way she should have all along.

The initial agreement had been a platonic marriage for a short term. Money would change hands. Everyone would get what they wanted. Instead she'd come up here in the middle of nowhere, stupidly looking for something that didn't exist. A happy ending. A fool wishing on stars. Now look where that had got her. She would have been lonely, but a hell of a lot happier if she'd stayed where she was.

The fact of the matter was, all Connor needed for the money was a marriage certificate. It didn't hinge on her actually *living* at Windover. Perhaps she should have insisted on that from the beginning. But she'd felt at home at the ranch, and she'd never questioned the decision to remain there until the baby was born. Until now. Why hadn't she thought of this before? She wasn't sure. But she was positive that, knowing her feelings, and knowing they were not returned in kind, she had to leave.

Connor pulled into the driveway and killed the engine. She hopped out, not waiting for him but using her own key to open the front door.

"Alex, wait," he called out from the foyer. She was already at the second step of the stairs.

He put his hand on the banister. "Are you OK?"

"I'm fine," she replied, taking another step.

"You don't sound fine. You don't *act* fine. I think we should talk about this."

"You want to talk? Be careful what you wish for, Connor. Because I'm still really angry."

"You don't hold the franchise on that, by the way." He bit the words back at her, hard verbal pellets. "I'd like to know exactly when I gave you the impression that you couldn't trust me."

She ignored the question, since she didn't have an answer. Instead she spun on the steps and marched back down to the bottom. "You know, we agreed to get married for your trust fund. You agreed to support me and the baby. That scenario doesn't require me to actually *live* here. I'm thinking it's probably best if I find my own place. I'll help out as much as I can if you'll give me some assistance with rent."

His mouth fell open in blatant shock. "Are you joking?"

"Not at all." He crowded her at the bottom of the stairs, close enough that she smelled the aftershave and dust and leather that made up the scent that was distinctly *Connor.* Even now, when she was spitting mad, hurt, and God knew what other emotion in the spectrum, just his smell had the power to bring to the surface all the longing she had for him. She pursed her lips and skirted around him, stalking toward the living room.

"It might be easier all around, rather than pretending that this is something it very clearly isn't."

The words echoed in a very sudden stillness, until his deep voice broke the awkward silence.

"Where would you go?" Already he felt how empty the house would be without her. The thought of her gone, even after so short a time, was like taking a living, breathing house and killing the pulse. In a few short weeks she'd made it a home again.

"It doesn't make sense," he continued. "It's ridiculous… Just take a deep breath and let your hormones settle, will you?"

"Hormones? You're going to blame this on *hormones?*"

Her mouth dropped open. She was incensed he'd even insinuate such a thing! "You don't understand anything, do you?"

She turned to run but he caught her by the forearm. "Then you'd better explain it to me. What's really going on?"

Her eyes blazed into his for a long moment. The words *I love you but you don't love me back* raced through her mind, but thankfully stopped at her lips. She took deep breaths, willing him to let go of her arm. When he didn't it took all the strength she had to answer quietly, deathly calm.

"From where I'm standing, it makes perfect sense. We both knew this plan was over the top to begin with. I'm not handling the strain well. I'm not good at pretending, Connor. I don't like lying. I can't do another six months of this."

If he thought she meant their agreement and *that* deception, well and good. It was better that he didn't know the pretending she meant was pretending not to love him when she did, so very desperately. She'd been humiliated enough. She wouldn't go a step further and make it worse by embarrassing him with flowery statements of unrequited devotion.

Connor withdrew, opened the patio doors and stepped out onto the deck. What was he going to do now? She'd already pulled away from him once; today she was suggesting she leave altogether. How could he explain how he felt now? It was obvious that her withdrawal the other night had been genuine. She didn't want him. He'd come on too strong the other night. He stared across the fields at the mountains, watched a hawk circling above, on the hunt for prairie dogs.

It wouldn't be fair to ask her to stay somewhere where she wasn't happy. But the option was life without her, and he couldn't accept that. Somehow he had to make her see that she could trust him. And trust him with her heart. He had to keep her here to do that.

He'd lost too many of those he'd loved. He wouldn't allow himself to lose another.

"Don't go," he whispered hoarsely, sensing her somewhere behind him. Somehow even the air changed when she was near. He knew he'd been right when she answered.

"I think I have to."

He turned his back on the peaks to the west and shook his head. "I'm sorry. I should have discussed it with you more before we went to the rodeo. I should have made sure you were comfortable with going. I…I hadn't thought out how I was going to answer questions about us. But I swear to you, Alexis, I didn't say anything about our arrangement."

"I felt so…cheap. Like everyone was looking and judging, even without knowing the truth."

Despite any fears, her words sparked something in him he could not ignore. He stepped forward and put his hands on her wrists. "Never. Not you. You are honorable and kind and good."

She pulled her hands away from his. "Someone honorable and good wouldn't have married for money."

"Someone honorable and good wouldn't have convinced a pregnant woman to marry him for a trust fund either."

"But that's why I should go—don't you see? At least if I leave it'll be honest."

He turned away from the earnest look on her face. Honest? Hardly. But the truth would send her running faster than any misapprehensions she was under now.

"I don't want you to go." He said it with his back to her. "That's honest."

"Why? Why does it matter where I live?"

"It just matters, OK?"

She'd looked like a scared jackrabbit the other night after he'd kissed her. If she knew he had real, deep feelings for her she'd panic and bolt. He knew that for sure now.

He kept his back to her as he tried what he could manage of an explanation. "I want you here. I want to know that you and the baby are fine. I enjoy your company, if it comes right down to it. I've rattled around in this old house for so long, having someone else here has spoiled me."

"I'm going eventually anyway. Why does it matter if it's now or in a few months?"

Connor turned and looked at her again. No matter how she protested, he could see her distress by the brightness of her eyes, the way her hand shook as it rested against the soft cotton of her top. She was upset—distraught, even. Now was not the time for her to be making rash decisions.

"You're far too upset right now to make any permanent decisions. I can't let you leave this way, Alex, I'm sorry."

He couldn't decipher the expression on her face. It had flattened with surprise, like she didn't quite know what to make of it.

"You're *forbidding* me?"

"For now, yes." He paused, gentling his voice. "Alex, I'm asking you to stay. To let this arrangement play out."

Oh, dear Lord. What was she going to do now? Her head said *go*. Staying any longer would only make leaving harder in the end. Staying and falling harder for him, knowing he didn't feel the same, would be torture.

She looked into his eyes. She'd never been able to resist his eyes; she should have known better. But in the moment their eyes met it was like she could hear him speaking, although his lips never moved.

Don't leave. Stay with me.

He might not be the biological father to her baby. And they had started out their relationship as strangers. But in her heart she also knew there was something more between them. Whether or not it was love, she couldn't be sure. But she did know there was a heart-to-heart recognition, and more—a need. They filled a need in each other. She gave the only answer she could possibly give.

"All right. I'll stay. For now."

* * *

The truce was a tentative one. It was like they both realized how tenuous a relationship they'd forged, one that could be easily damaged, even broken. They walked on eggshells around each other, keeping to the most inane pleasantries. In the following days there were no more intimate rocks on the porch swing, no more kisses in the moonlight or long looks across the breakfast table. It was, in fact, very much like they'd both envisioned in the beginning. Friendly. Amicable. Completely and absolutely platonic.

Alex alternated between being glad she'd stayed and being angry at herself for not having the fortitude to leave.

Connor was friendly, what she would assume was his normal happy self. He smiled and joked at mealtimes, enquired solicitously how she was feeling, made plans for the ranch when the money came through.

But she missed their intimacy terribly.

She held back too. She took pleasure in keeping the house scrubbed and shined, improved her cooking by sheer force of will, and picked the very first greens from the garden—the first she'd ever grown on her own. But there were no more languid looks from across the room, and when the baby kicked she smiled to herself and ran her hand over her tummy reassuringly. She didn't reach for his hand to feel too, and she missed the warmth of his wide palm on her taut skin.

She didn't ask any more about the crisis with the ranch. Instead they lived each day the same, no peaks, no valleys.

The second Tuesday in July dawned already swelteringly hot. Alex woke with the covers already thrown off. Since it was only six a.m., and the air was already like an oven, she dressed in shorts, a light halter top and her sandals.

Her eyes strayed to the picture on the night table. She'd taken it out of her backpack the night before the wedding and placed it beside her bed. It was the only picture she'd ever saved and bothered to carry with her. In a plain wood frame was a five-by-seven family picture—her, her mother and father, in a studio-type shot. Tucked behind the colour photo in the back of the frame were two newspaper articles. One was a copy of the same picture, and a small story from an Ottawa paper on her parents and one of their adventures. She had been thirteen at the time.

The other article was an extended obituary for her parents after the crash, outlining their achievements.

She'd garnered a whole line in that one. Even with their death, she'd still felt like she'd been less of an achievement than their career.

Alex put her hair up in a ponytail, twisting the tail around and around and anchoring the dark bun with a plain band, keeping her neck free and hopefully cool. When she was done she placed both hands over the place where her child lay. And she vowed that her baby would always know what was important. That nothing mattered more than him or her. For a while she'd indulged in fantasies about how Connor would look, cradling her child in his arms, kissing its tiny fingers one by one. Now she had to adjust those visions to something more realistic…her and motherhood, and making sure her child always felt loved and valued.

Connor was already gone when she went downstairs, so she ate a quick breakfast, washed a load of towels and decided to pick vegetables out of the garden before the heat became unbearable.

When Connor came in at noon he carried the mail.

"Anything good?" Alex finished setting the table and put out a plate of sandwiches and a bowl of fresh greens and tomatoes.

Connor slit open the first envelope. "It's the bank confirmation. My trust fund went through. I officially am in the black." He couldn't hold back the relief in his voice at finally being able to pay the bills. On the other hand, he wasn't sure what this meant for his relationship with Alex.

She'd married him for the security. He couldn't deceive himself on that point. She'd made it abundantly clear in every way possible. A farmer's life was unpredictable, hard, and even lonely. He couldn't expect her to choose this indefinitely. Even if he did want her to. Knowing she was there when he got home, seeing her laugh, cry, argue…all had him feeling more alive than he had in years. She was right. The place would seem empty when it was just him rattling around in it again.

He was too used to losing people he cared about. The last time he hadn't foreseen enough to try to prevent it.

This time he could see trouble coming from a mile away. Connor remembered the feeling he'd had when the baby had moved beneath his hand. Protective. Humbled. Strong. What would it be like to have a son or daughter? To hear it cry and soothe it with a rock in the rocking chair, to see the baby feed at its mother's breast in the pale light of early morning?

He was wishing this was his family, his baby, and he had absolutely no right. He knew that if Alex gave him a chance he'd be a father to her baby, blood or no. If he felt this way after only a few weeks, how would he feel after the baby was born and he had to set her free? There had to be some way he could give her a reason to stay long enough for him to prove to her that he could be what she needed. What she *wanted*.

"That's great," Alex answered weakly. "Sit down and eat. I'll get you some water."

Connor held a ham sandwich with one hand and bit into it while he sorted through the remainder of envelopes with the other.

"Connor? What is it?"

He had stopped chewing, and the hand holding the sandwich put it down like it weighed five pounds. He picked up a brown envelope, staring at the front.

"Connor?"

When he looked at her she saw something new in his eyes—a real fear. Her stomach tumbled. Whatever was in that envelope wasn't good.

"Open it," she whispered.

He ran his finger under the seal and pulled out the papers inside. His tanned face paled; his lips thinned until they were white around the edges.

Suddenly he started laughing. Not a funny laugh, but the frightening laugh of a man who'd reached the end of his rope. Like one who'd finally lost his hold on reality.

"Connor. You're scaring me." Her voice trembled as she stared at him, her lips falling open as the laughter halted as quickly as it had begun.

"It's over," he said flatly. His eyes were dull as he stared up at her. "We're linked, you see. No trust fund in the world can help me now."

"What are you talking about?" She took a step forward, halting at his look of sheer despair.

His next words broke her heart as surely as they had broken his spirit.

"I've got to cull the herd. Windover's done."

CHAPTER FOURTEEN

"OH, MY God. No."

Alex sank into her chair, staring blankly at Connor. His face showed no reaction, which scared her most of all. It was like someone had turned off a switch. It had to be shock.

"They've traced the lineage of the affected animal. There's a direct tie to Windover. The herd. My God. The whole herd," he breathed, stricken.

He looked at her with eyes so haunted she knew she'd never forget it as long as she lived.

Windover. The one thing he would do anything for. Any extreme measure…even marrying a pregnant stranger. The one thing linking him to his lost family. The one permanent fixture in his life. His sole responsibility.

Without livestock there *was* no Windover. She didn't have to be a true rancher's wife to know that much.

"So you rebuild," she offered. "You try something else, or replace the herd. You don't give up."

He stared at her. "Don't give up? How the hell would I replace the herd? Do you know how much time and money it takes to build a herd like that?"

She didn't, and the blank look on her face said so.

He snorted. "Do something else." He muttered it almost to himself.

"In the end, it's fate," he continued, his tone bitter and angry. "It doesn't matter how much you do, how hard you try. It doesn't matter."

"Don't say that!" Sitting in her chair, she reached over and gripped his fingers. "At least you know you tried everything. What happened is out of your control!"

"Exactly." He looked at her, and she could have sworn there was something like accusation in his glare. "Everything's out of my control now."

"Don't panic. We'll figure it out somehow."

Alex did something she would never have imagined herself doing. At twelve-thirty in the afternoon, she went to the cupboard, took out the tequila, and poured him a double shot.

For a moment he stared at the amber liquid, but in the end he pushed it away and looked up into her eyes.

She didn't have a clue, did she? All he'd wanted was to show her that he could make this work. That it would be worth it for her to stay.

She thought it was the cows he was upset about. She was wrong. Dead wrong.

It was her. Without the ranch, without the trust fund, without Windover, he had nothing to offer her. Sometime over the last weeks he'd started caring for something other than Windover. Finally, after years of being alone, something, someone, mattered more. He'd started doing it all for *her.* For Alex and her baby. And all he'd done was fail spectacularly.

In that moment he hated her just a bit, for making him love again so much and then making him lose.

"You have no idea what you're talking about, anyway," he accused. "You came here from the city. You don't understand ranch life. You don't understand what all this means to a man like me. You asked me what in our agreement required you to be here. The answer is nothing, Alex. Absolutely nothing. You might as well go back where you came from."

Ignoring the bottle, he stood and headed for the front door. "Stop."

His footsteps halted at the harsh command, but he didn't turn around.

When nothing came from her he wondered. Wondered what he'd see when he turned around. Lord, if she were crying he might as well pound himself in the head with a two-by-four. It would hurt less. He'd lashed out at her but wasn't prepared yet to apologize. Everything was too fresh, too raw. His failures. His inability to make things right. Even this baby wasn't his. He was like a big walking advertisement for complete impotence.

"If that's what you want, I'll pack my things."

Her voice came quietly from behind him, and he forced himself to ignore the strange thickness to it. Her emotions were riding close to the surface, and right now he could only deal with his own.

"I've gotta get out of here," he answered, reaching for the doorknob.

"You can't. Please, Connor, I've never seen you like this. In your frame of mind, I'll worry about you driving."

He held the doorknob in his hand. "I'm just going to take the ATV, not the truck," he replied.

"Please don't," she begged. "You're not thinking clearly… you might hurt yourself."

Finally he turned, staring at her with hard eyes, his face a series of angles that spoke pain.

"And would you care, Alexis?"

She gasped, stepping back with her fingers over her mouth. With a searing backward glance he went out, slamming the front door behind him.

Mere seconds later the motor of the quad revved, grinding into gear and fading away as Connor headed north.

Alex went back to the kitchen, her muscles knotted with

worry. He was in no condition to drive. He was in such a fragile state right now.

Everything he held dear—his purpose for everything—was being snatched away from him. And she was powerless to stop it.

If only he'd loved her she could have offered comfort, solace. She'd maybe have known what he needed and been able to offer it. But instead he'd taken it out on her, when all she'd wanted was to help.

She poured the tequila down the sink and recapped the bottle. Yes, she was from the city and hadn't had years of ranch experience. And, no, she wasn't that up to snuff with the logistics of it all. But she knew a damn sight more than he thought. She knew what this place meant. She knew he felt like a failure, and she knew he'd regret it forever if he gave up without seeing it through.

She'd offered help. And he'd pushed her away with hurtful words and an impenetrable emotional wall. Never in her life had she felt so superfluous.

If he couldn't see what was standing right in front of him, that was his problem. She wasn't going to stand around begging. She should have packed her things the day of the rodeo. Instead she'd stayed and opened herself up to more hurt.

Now he was *out there* somewhere, driving balls to the wall on a four-wheeler. She stared at their uneaten lunch, knowing that the time had come for this charade to be over.

She was not his wife, not really. And very clearly she was not what he needed. She grabbed the laundry basket and stepped out to the deck to take her clean clothes off the line before she packed them. He was right. There was nothing to keep her here now.

She pushed back the tendrils of hair that had escaped her bun, breathing deeply. The air had changed somehow. Suddenly the sweltering heat carried a threatening icy chill.

She gazed north, eyeing the clouds curiously. Something was wrong. The clouds were piling layer upon layer and growing darker by the minute. The sun shone on her back, but in front of her the clouds approached, menacing. She saw a flash—lightning. Several seconds later came the low rumble of answering thunder.

Connor must see the weather, she reasoned, figuring him to be back soon. Surely he wouldn't ignore the signs he sensed so easily at other times? She reeled in the line, watching open-mouthed as a gust of icy wind yanked a dishcloth off its pins and sent it tumbling down the farmyard.

She hurriedly took the rest of the clothes down and went back inside. As she put lunch back in the fridge and tidied up the kitchen, the rumble of thunder grew closer, louder. A gust of wind came through the patio doors, flapping the vertical blinds. She jumped at the harsh sound, trying to steady her racing heart.

It took all of ten minutes to pack her things. There were extra clothes this time, a plastic bag of toiletries and her picture to put back among the clothing to protect it. For lack of luggage, she retrieved a cardboard box from the basement and laid her wedding finery carefully within it. Anger and resentment burned within her. Connor had succeeded in doing what everyone else had done before him. He'd made her feel like she wasn't worth it.

Well, maybe she wasn't. But her baby darn well was. Connor would live up to his bargain in that he'd help her get on her feet. After that she'd be alone again…but wiser and stronger. She carried the box downstairs and waited.

After a half-hour of pacing and mumbling to herself, she went back out on the deck, scanning the pasture to the north anxiously. Connor should have been back by now. The clouds were dark, and the odd colour of an angry bruise. She put a hand to her eyes and searched the horizon for any sight of him.

Nothing. The sun had disappeared and the first angry drop of rain hit her forehead as she looked up, up.

Lightning forked from the sky, this time the thunder almost on top of it. The storm was getting closer. Alex ran a hand over her belly, trying to comfort herself and her baby. As if it sensed something was amiss, the kicks got stronger and more frequent.

"Shh, little one," she whispered, her eyes never leaving the dirt road through the fields, willing Connor to return any moment. "Daddy'll be back soon."

Once the words were out she knew it was true. Ryan had fathered this baby, but he wasn't Daddy. Connor, with his gentle ways, his quiet strength, was meant to be Daddy to her baby, and somehow she had to make him see that. All her anger flooded away, replaced by concern. Connor was devastated, and that had colored everything he'd said, surely? All the animosity had simply been a reaction. She didn't really feel that way about him—she loved him. And if he thought he would get rid of her that easily…

Her hand stopped circling her belly as her mouth dropped open in horror. It couldn't be…no.

She watched as the swirling clouds changed and a funnel, like the circle of water in the bathtub, pointed down from the clouds, reaching for the earth.

She waited, hoping to see that destructive finger sucked back into the clouds. Instead it reached, reached, until she saw it hit the earth, gathering speed and dust and momentum.

It was close, too close. She cried out as ice-sharp hail bit into her skin and the swirling vortex came closer and closer.

"Oh, my God—oh, my God," she chanted, horrified that Connor was out there. The hail pounded her now, the size of peas from the garden, and she hurried inside.

The wind wailed around the house and she let fear be her guide. All her instincts said to head for the cellar. Alone, in the dark, she huddled beside the Deepfreeze and the wooden shelves, waiting for the storm to be over.

It lasted only ten minutes, but each minute was a lifetime in which she knew without a doubt that she loved Connor with all her heart. Each wail of the wind solidified the knowledge that she was meant to be with him, Windover or not. Each rattle of the windows, each foundation-shaking boom of thunder, told her that nothing in the world was more important than loving him, fighting for him, and bringing up her child with him at her side.

Pride be damned. There'd been enough pride today to fill up ten ranches. Right then and there she made a vow to tell him exactly how she felt.

The wind subsided a bit, the thunder grew more distant, and she crept upstairs to view the aftermath.

Once the funnel had passed by, the rain came in its wake. It was coming down in sheets, cold, driving rain instead of the earlier hail that had preceded the tornado. Numbly she pulled on an old fleece coat of Connor's that hung on the hook by the door. Stepping outside, she covered her mouth in horror at the sight before her.

The house remained untouched, but evidence of the twister was clear.

The poplar, the one under which they'd been married, was gone, it's branches lying scattered and it's trunk shorn completely off, a circle of ragged edges. The outbuildings were in a varying state of disarray. Pieces of roofing were scattered throughout the barnyard; the livestock shelter at the southeast side of the corral was splintered.

Her hair came completely loose from its tether, hanging wildly around her face in the driving rain. She stumbled down the drive, heading north. He'd gone north, she reasoned stupidly, beginning to run. The twister had come from the north.

She forgot the mud splattering over her sandals. Forgot the

rain soaking through her clothes and matting her hair. Forgot how dirt smacked up and coated her bare legs.

She only thought of Connor, unprotected, devastated, in such a storm.

"Connor!" she called out as she ran across the road and into the next quarter section.

There was no answer to her call.

She placed a hand instinctively where her baby lay, but kept running. "Connor!"

She ran and ran, but heard no voice, no engine. Her lungs were on fire from running, her abdominals cramping from exertion. "Connor!" she screamed one last time.

She turned in a circle, searching the fields, seeing nothing but matted-down grass and mud.

Nothing.

She stood in the middle of the lane, dropped her head, and finally gave in to the tears she'd been holding in.

Damn him. He'd probably gone and done something completely stupid right at the moment she'd decided to tell him exactly how she felt! The tears came hot and fast even as the rain tapered off, steady and cool. What would she do without him?

Blindly she staggered on, until suddenly she saw a dark green form to the left. Crying, slipping and sliding in the slick black mud, she raced for the quad—only to discover he wasn't there.

He'd left the quad there, with the key in it.

She cradled the soft mound of her stomach beneath his jacket, sinking down and resting her head on the foot peg. In the damp she caught *his* smell rising up from the fleece, and her heart broke. How could he have the nerve to leave her now, just when she was ready to confess everything in her heart?

"I'm sorry," she sobbed, resting her head on the cold metal bar. "I'm sorry…"

"Alex?"

Her head slipped down until she was huddled on the muddy ground, crying uncontrollably. A cow bawled in the distance and she cursed at it, thinking of the injustice that a stupid bovine should live while Connor was out there... After seeing the state of the barn, she knew that no man, unprotected, could survive such a thing.

"Alex?"

"Shut up!" she screamed at the clouds. Now she was hearing things!

"Oh, my God, Alex—what the hell are you doing out here?"

This time there was no mistaking it, and she lifted her head to see Connor running toward the quad.

She tried to speak, she did. But no words would come out. Instead she cried even harder, knowing he was alive. The sobs turned into hysterical, hyperventilating quality wails as she huddled into a ball in the mud.

"Alex, honey—oh, God. Look at you."

She gasped in a huge breath of air, lifted her head, and smacked the cheek hovering close to her own.

"What the hell was that for?" He leaned back, pressing a hand to his red cheek.

She stumbled to her feet. "For scaring me to death, you jerk! For breaking your promise!"

All of her anger faded with the outburst, the adrenaline sapped out of her. She gripped the fingers of her right hand, horrified at what she'd done. "Oh, Connor, I'm so sorry I slapped you!"

She covered her mouth and started sobbing again.

"Hey, I'm all right," he said soothingly, while raindrops dripped from his hair. "What promise?"

She looked up, wide eyes imploring him to understand. "You promised you wouldn't hurt me. The night before the wedding. Our temporary vows, remember? You said you wouldn't be the one to hurt me."

"And I did?"

She looked down at her feet. How could he be so blind? She was covered in mud splatters to her knees. Her jacket was soaked and hanging on her, and her hair drooped around her face. "Of course you did! Look at me! I'm a mess! I came out here looking for you and for what? You have the nerve to stand there looking like that!"

"Looking like what?"

"Like some hero from an action movie, that's what!"

Why couldn't she do what she'd promised herself and tell him?

Because he was living and breathing in front of her, that was why. And it still scared her to death. So she instinctively wrapped herself in some ridiculous armor to protect herself.

"Alex?"

"What?" She glared at him through the driving rain.

"I have the power to hurt you?"

"Why does that matter?" She huddled inside the jacket, which was already soaked.

"It matters to me."

"Why?"

"Because I love you."

It took six giant strides to meet her, but when he did he swept her, mud and all, into his arms and kissed her.

It was Rhett and Scarlett. It was Darcy and Elizabeth, and every romance hero ever written and rolled into one. Rain beat down on their heads as they clung, lips greedy.

"I was so scared," she cried out, pressing kisses to his cheeks, his chin. "I saw the tornado coming and knew you were out here..."

"I tried coming back. I did," he stuttered out. "But it came too fast. I left the quad and took cover in the culvert, but all I thought of was you and the baby..."

"You shouldn't have run out..."

"I should never have said those things…"

They kissed again, a swift meeting of tongues and lips, and the baby kicked between them and they laughed from the sheer joy of it.

"Say it again."

He pulled back, staring into her eyes. "You really want me to?"

"Say it. I need to hear it again to know it's real."

"I love you, Alexis MacKenzie Madsen."

The tears started again. "I love you too, Connor. I just never thought you'd love me back."

He drew her close. "How could I not?"

For a long moment she let herself be wrapped into his arms. Finally she stepped back, shuddering.

"You're freezing. We've got to get you out of this rain."

She didn't argue, but crawled up behind him on the quad and wrapped her arms around his waist. He turned the key…nothing.

"What next?" He cursed at the machine and tried again, but no luck. It wasn't starting. They were going to have to walk.

He helped her off the ATV and bundled her close. "What were you thinking, coming all the way out there in the rain? You're going to get sick."

She stopped him with a tug of her hand. "I was thinking I'd lost you."

Their steps made squishy sounds along the path, the mud caking on their shoes. "I didn't mean it when I said you should go. I was frustrated."

"I know that."

"I was in that culvert, and it was so loud I couldn't have heard my own voice. But I knew that if I made it out I had to tell you I was sorry. That I lied about my feelings."

"You're not sending me away?"

He lifted a hand to her cheek. "Never. I'm tired of pretending, Alex. I think I've loved you since that first moment."

"You're crazy. There's no such thing as love at first sight, you fool."

"I'm not." He squeezed her close. "You opened your eyes and looked into mine and something *happened*."

"I packed my bags after you left."

His face hardened in alarm as she stopped and faced him, looking up into his eyes.

She stopped his protest with gentle words. "I'd like very much to unpack and start over. The right way."

"Then you meant it? You love me too?" He swallowed hard. She saw the lump bob in his throat and wanted to lean up and kiss it.

"I knew the night before our wedding. When you made your vows to me. I knew I was falling for you and was sure you didn't feel the same. It made marrying you very surreal, Connor Madsen."

"It felt real," he admitted. He took her hand and urged her on, in view of the house now.

"I want to make promises to you—the real ones this time."

"Another wedding?"

"Not so much…but real vows, to you. The things I wanted to say, but didn't. I want to do this right. Things have a way of becoming very clear when you think you've lost someone. Like I thought I'd lost you."

Without another word he turned, gathered her, soaking wet, into his arms, and held on.

Long seconds they clung, each taking strength from the other, while the rain tapered to drizzle and a weak bit of sunlight snuck out between the clouds behind them.

"This is not how I expected to spend my afternoon," he commented as they resumed walking.

It suddenly occurred to her that he didn't know that the buildings had been hit. "Connor, about the tornado…"

He saw the house, obviously still standing. "How bad?"

"The southeast shelter and the corral fence are gone. So's the poplar, and the barn and other buildings looked like they have a lot of roof damage." She gave it to him all at once, knowing he'd take it easier that way.

"It doesn't matter—since I'm not going to have any livestock to put in them anyway."

Her head fell heavily against his shoulder. She was feeling so sorry for his loss. He'd worked himself into the ground only to have it torn away from him. "I'm sorry about the herd, Connor. I wish there was something I could do."

He stiffened, then let out a breath. "You're doing it."

It wasn't much, but in that moment she was closer to him than she'd ever been. In that moment he was letting himself lean on her, and she knew if he truly meant what he said they'd make a wonderful team.

"We'll make it through," she confirmed. "Somehow we'll figure it out."

He angled his head away so that he saw her face, strong with determination. "You mean you're staying? Even when I've lost everything? I don't think you understand what it means to have to cull the herd. Windover as I know it…as it's been for generations…is done."

She half turned, snuggling into his shoulder and looking up at him. Her jaw set with determination and she wrapped an arm around his waist for good measure.

"What do you mean, done? You've got a huge, fabulous piece of land, a beautiful house, and most of all you've got your biggest asset—you. So you don't have a herd of beef cattle for the moment? You'll figure out something else and we'll go from there."

He shook his head. "I would never have guessed it."

"Guessed what?"

"That you were a rancher's wife."

She grinned then, wide and happy. "Me either. Go figure."

They stepped into the lane that ran to the house. She looked up at the building, so much more than a house. The first home she'd ever really had, the first place she'd belonged since she could remember. Her vegetable garden on the corner, thriving despite her green attempts. There was blue sky behind them now, while the dark clouds continued their journey to the southeast.

Their home. One that had survived other tragedies and was still standing.

"All I've ever wanted was a place to belong, and someone to belong to."

"This house was meant for families, not bachelors bumbling around by themselves." His arms tightened around her. "Stay with me Alex. Love me. Family me."

"I thought you'd never ask." Alex leaned up, touched her lips to his, while she pressed her body as close to his as their damp clothes would allow.

They reached the door. He swung it open, then shocked her by gathering her, wet coat and all, into his arms and carrying her inside.

He murmured in her ear. "Maybe I wouldn't do this for myself. I probably would have given up and let go, despite the family tradition of hanging on. But for you…for the future…I know I have the strength to rebuild. Because you're with me."

Alex had to swallow the tears that gathered in the back of her throat. "We've needed each other all along," she whispered, curling around him and kissing him again.

EPILOGUE

One Year Later

"GO AHEAD, say it. Da-da."

Maren Johanna Madsen grinned up with her two teeth and drooled. "Da-da-da-da-da."

"Very definitive. A sign of high intelligence, I'm sure."

Alex leaned over the highchair, kissing the crown of her daughter's dark head. Connor lounged back in his chair while Johanna came from the pantry carrying a gigantic chocolate layer cake.

"Go ahead, Maren, say Grandma," she cajoled, with an affectionate grin.

"Da-da-da-da-da," Maren babbled happily.

Johanna smiled widely, putting the cake on the table and cutting it into slices. "Now, there's a girl who knows where her heart lies, hmm?" She couldn't resist stopping and tickling Maren's belly.

A year had passed since the slaughter decree and the tornado. A lot had changed since then. Connor's friend Mike had stopped running the rodeo circuit and had seriously started breeding quarterhorses by renting a large portion of Windover. Connor had accepted Mike's offer of a partnership in the venture. Maren had been born, and Alex had shown a talent for running an office…so all the records for Circle M Quarterhorses were in her control.

She picked up a sheaf of documents from the counter as Connor leaned back, enjoying cake and coffee. "These came today," she announced. "Although it's merely a formality."

"What is it?"

"Maren's adoption papers."

They'd filed after Maren was born, and Ryan hadn't contested a thing—thankfully. Now their sweet baby girl was officially what she'd always been in his heart—his daughter.

Johanna stopped and put her plate back on the counter as soon as she saw the look on Connor's face. His eyes caught Alex's and held, so full of emotion and love that to stay would have been intruding.

She slipped away, leaving them alone.

The screen door shut quietly while Connor rose, his gaze never straying from the loving eyes of his wife.

"So now she's ours."

"She always was. As much as this one will be."

"What?"

"I'd like a boy this time. But I suppose we'll have to be happy with what we get," she teased.

"One of each would be good," he mused, pulling her close and tucking her head under his chin. "But we can always try again…"

"And again…"

"Until we get it right…"

"Like right now…" He nuzzled her neck and she sighed, only to hear Maren's spoon banging against her tray. Alex craned her head around and smiled at the baby.

"You're really pregnant?"

"I am. Only this time I'm healthy as a horse."

Connor spun around, plucked Maren from her highchair,

banana face and all, and swung them both around. "And this time there's no wild propositions," he decreed. "This time you're both exactly where you belong. With me."

* * * * *

Mediterranean Nights

Join the guests and crew of Alexandra's Dream, *the newest luxury ship to set sail on the romantic Mediterranean, as they experience the glamorous world of cruising.*

*A new Harlequin continuity series
begins in June 2007 with
FROM RUSSIA, WITH LOVE
by Ingrid Weaver*

Marina Artamova *books a cabin on the luxurious cruise ship* Alexandra's Dream, *when she finds out that her orphaned nephew and his adoptive father are aboard. She's determined to be reunited with the boy…but the romantic ambience of the ship and her undeniable attraction to a man she considers her enemy are about to interfere with her quest!*

Turn the page for a sneak preview!

...why two canoes since they had left the main paddle, ...
...it was probably because of the boat...according to the...

Piraeus, Greece

"THERE SHE IS, Stefan. *Alexandra's Dream*." David Anderson squatted beside his new son and pointed at the dark blue hull that towered above the pier. The cruise ship was a majestic sight, twelve decks high and as long as a city block. A circle of silver and gold stars, the logo of the Liberty Cruise Line, gleamed from the swept-back smokestack. Like some legendary sea creature born for the water, the ship emanated power from every sleek curve—even at rest it held the promise of motion. "That's going to be our home for the next ten days."

The child beside him remained silent, his cheeks working in and out as he sucked furiously on his thumb. Hair so blond it appeared white ruffled against his forehead in the harbor breeze. The baby-sweet scent unique to the very young mingled with the tang of the sea.

"Ship," David said. "Uh, *parakhod*."

From beneath his bangs, Stefan looked at the *Alexandra's Dream*. Although he didn't release his thumb, the corners of his mouth tightened with the beginning of a smile.

David grinned. That was Stefan's first smile this afternoon, one of only two since they had left the orphanage yesterday. It was probably because of the boat—according to the orphanage staff, the boy loved boats, which was the main reason David had decided to book this cruise. Then again, there was a strong possibility the smile could have been a reaction to David's attempt at pocket-dictionary Russian. Whatever the cause, it was a good start.

The liaison from the adoption agency had claimed that Stefan had been taught some English, but David had yet to see evidence of it. David continued to speak, positive his son would understand his tone even if he couldn't grasp the words. "This is her maiden voyage. Her first trip, just like this is our first trip, and that makes it special." He motioned toward the stage that had been set up on the pier beneath the ship's bow. "That's why everyone's celebrating."

The ship's official christening ceremony had been held the day before and had been a closed affair, with only the cruise-line executives and VIP guests invited, but the stage hadn't yet been disassembled. Banners bearing the blue and white of the Greek flag of the ship's owner, as well as the Liberty circle of stars logo, draped the edges of the platform. In the center, a group of musicians and a dance troupe dressed in traditional white folk costumes performed for the benefit of the *Alexandra's Dream*'s first passengers. Their audience was in a festive mood, snapping their fingers in time to the music while the dancers twirled and wove through their steps.

David bobbed his head to the rhythm of the mandolins. They were playing a folk tune that seemed vaguely familiar, possibly from a movie he'd seen. He hummed a few notes. "Catchy melody, isn't it?"

Stefan turned his gaze on David. His eyes were a striking shade of blue, as cool and pale as a winter horizon and far too solemn for a child not yet five. Still, the smile that hovered at the corners of his mouth persisted. He moved his head with the music, mirroring David's motion.

David gave a silent cheer at the interaction. Hopefully, this cruise would provide countless opportunities for more. "Hey, good for you," he said. "Do you like the music?"

The child's eyes sparked. He withdrew his thumb with a pop. *"Moozika!"*

"Music. Right!" David held out his hand. "Come on, let's go closer so we can watch the dancers."

Stefan grasped David's hand quickly, as if he feared it would be withdrawn. In an instant his budding smile was replaced by a look close to panic.

Did he remember the car accident that had killed his parents? It would be a mercy if he didn't. As far as David knew, Stefan had never spoken of it to anyone. Whatever he had seen had made him run so far from the crash that the police hadn't found him until the next day. The event had traumatized him to the extent that he hadn't uttered a word until his fifth week at the orphanage. Even now he seldom talked.

David sat back on his heels and brushed the hair from Stefan's forehead. That solemn, too-old gaze locked with his, and for an instant, David felt as if he looked back in time at an image of himself thirty years ago.

He didn't need to speak the same language to understand exactly how this boy felt. He knew what it meant to be alone and powerless among strangers, trying to be brave and tough but wishing with every fiber of his being for a place to belong, to be safe, and most of all for someone to love him....

He knew in his heart he would be a good parent to Stefan. It was why he had never considered halting the adoption process after Ellie had left him. He hadn't balked when he'd learned of the recent claim by Stefan's spinster aunt, either; the absentee relative had shown up too late for her case to be considered. The adoption was meant to be. He and this child already shared a bond that went deeper than paperwork or legalities.

A seagull screeched overhead, making Stefan start and press closer to David.

"That's my boy," David murmured. He swallowed hard, struck by the simple truth of what he had just said.

That's my *boy.*

"I CAN'T BE PATIENT, RUDOLPH. I'm not going to stand by and watch my nephew get ripped from his country and his roots to live on the other side of the world."

Rudolph hissed out a slow breath. "Marina, I don't like the sound of that. What are you planning?"

"I'm going to talk some sense into this American kidnapper."

"No. Absolutely not. No offence, but diplomacy is not your strong suit."

"Diplomacy be damned. Their ship's due to sail at five o'clock."

"Then you wouldn't have an opportunity to speak with him even if his lawyer agreed to a meeting."

"I'll have ten days of opportunities, Rudolph, since I plan to be on board that ship."

* * * * *

Follow Marina and David as they join forces to uncover the reason behind little Stefan's unusual silence, and the secret behind the death of his parents....

Look for From Russia, With Love by Ingrid Weaver in stores June 2007.

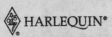

HARLEQUIN®

American ROMANCE®

is proud to present a special treat this
Fourth of July with three stories
to kick off your summer!

SUMMER LOVIN'
by
Marin Thomas,
Laura Marie Altom
Ann Roth

This year, celebrating the Fourth of July in Silver Cliff,
Colorado, is going to be special. There's an all-year
high school reunion taking place before the old
school building gets torn down. As old flames find
each other and new romances begin, this small
town is looking like the perfect place
for some summer lovin'!

Available June 2007
wherever Harlequin books are sold.

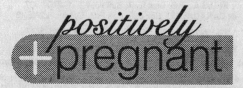

REQUEST YOUR FREE BOOKS!
2 FREE NOVELS PLUS 2
FREE GIFTS!

HARLEQUIN ROMANCE®

From the Heart, For the Heart

YES! Please send me 2 FREE Harlequin Romance® novels and my 2 FREE gifts. After receiving them, if I don't wish to receive any more books, I can return the shipping statement marked "cancel." If I don't cancel, I will receive 4 brand-new novels every month and be billed just $3.57 per book in the U.S., or $4.05 per book in Canada, plus 25¢ shipping and handling per book and applicable taxes, if any*. That's a savings of over 15% off the cover price! I understand that accepting the 2 free books and gifts places me under no obligation to buy anything. I can always return a shipment and cancel at any time. Even if I never buy another book from Harlequin, the two free books and gifts are mine to keep forever.

114 HDN EEV7 314 HDN EEWK

Name _____ (PLEASE PRINT) _____

Address _____ Apt. _____

City _____ State/Prov. _____ Zip/Postal Code _____

Signature (if under 18, a parent or guardian must sign)

Mail to the **Harlequin Reader Service®**:
IN U.S.A.: P.O. Box 1867, Buffalo, NY 14240-1867
IN CANADA: P.O. Box 609, Fort Erie, Ontario L2A 5X3

Not valid to current Harlequin Romance subscribers.

Want to try two free books from another line?
Call 1-800-873-8635 or visit www.morefreebooks.com.

* Terms and prices subject to change without notice. NY residents add applicable sales tax. Canadian residents will be charged applicable provincial taxes and GST. This offer is limited to one order per household. All orders subject to approval. Credit or debit balances in a customer's account(s) may be offset by any other outstanding balance owed by or to the customer. Please allow 4 to 6 weeks for delivery.

Your Privacy: Harlequin is committed to protecting your privacy. Our Privacy Policy is available online at www.eHarlequin.com or upon request from the Reader Service. From time to time we make our lists of customers available to reputable firms who may have a product or service of interest to you. If you would prefer we not share your name and address, please check here. ☐

HR07

HARLEQUIN *Romance*

Coming Next Month

#3955 A MOTHER FOR THE TYCOON'S CHILD Patricia Thayer
Rocky Mountain Brides
Dedicated Mayor Morgan Keenan has no time for love. It takes newcomer tycoon and caring single father Justin Hilliard to see past Morgan's defenses and help heal her painful past. Can Justin show Morgan that she's meant to be his adored wife and a mother?

#3956 THE BOSS AND HIS SECRETARY Jessica Steele
When Taryn Webster takes a job with gorgeous millionaire Jake Nash, she is determined not to mix business and pleasure. But then Jake asks her for help out of hours! At first Taryn refuses, but she can't resist his persuasive arguments—nor his charming smile and tempting gray eyes.

#3957 THE SHEIKH'S CONTRACT BRIDE Teresa Southwick
Brothers of Bha'Khar
Sheikh Malik Hourani, Crown Prince of Bha'Khar, is a rich and powerful man, dedicated to ruling his kingdom—but experience has made him wary of love. Beautiful Beth Farrar has been betrothed to the sheikh since birth, but she has a secret! She's not the woman he thinks she is.

#3958 MARRIED BY MORNING Shirley Jump
Makeover Bride & Groom
When playboy Carter Matthews decides to prove his reliability by getting married, his ever-practical employee Daphne thinks his idea is ridiculous. Especially when she discovers that she's his chosen bride-to-be! Will Carter and Daphne be married by morning?

#3959 BILLIONAIRE ON HER DOORSTEP Ally Blake
Billionaire Tom Campbell is content with his pace of life in sleepy Sorrento. Then he walks up to the doorstep of Maggie Bryce's ramshackle mansion, and he can see both are in need of some loving care. Maggie's alluring mystique captures the billionaire's heart and he can't let go.

#3960 PRINCESS AUSTRALIA Nicola Marsh
By Royal Appointment
Natasha Telford is an everyday Australian girl. Dante Andretti is gorgeous, charming…and a prince! They couldn't be more different. But Dante needs her help and Natasha is just the ordinary girl he's looking for. Maybe she has what it takes to be his extraordinary princess!

HRCNM0507